哈福

第一本聽力會話自學書

世界最強 英文聽力會話

LC Made Easy In 30 Days

蘇盈盈—著

附 MP3

一次學好聽力 & 會話

▶ 【本書 7 大特色】

1. 一次學好聽力 & 會話
2. 英語聽力口語強化練習
3. 高效訓練耳朵的聽力
4. 打開耳朵，每天 10 分鐘
5. 英語聽力會話全速起飛
6. 快速提高您的英文聽力、會話
7. 英語能力從 C 到 A⁺，迅速升級

▶ 【最大 5 優勢】

奇蹟式的激發你的英語本能

1. 為什麼文法書背到頭昏腦脹？
2. 為什麼看到老外仍結結巴巴？
3. 本書以有趣的會話取代枯燥文法
4. 火速搶救您的聽力和口說能力
5. 30 天讓您的英語更上一層樓

▶ 【連老鼠都要學狗叫】

一隻母老鼠帶著幾隻小老鼠在草地裡漫步,忽然間,來了一隻貓咪,小老鼠個個都嚇得躲了起來,只有母老鼠沉著冷靜,沒有躲開。眼看著貓咪越走越近,小老鼠們非常害怕,就在這時,母老鼠叫了一聲:bark!(英語裡的狗叫聲)貓一聽,就調頭跑了。於是母老鼠語重心長地說:『孩子們,現在知道學英語的重要性了吧!』

雖然這只是一則網路笑話,但我們都知道,英語學習在全球化的潮流中已是不可阻擋的趨勢。不只是亞洲,連一向為自己的母語引以為傲的德、法等歐洲國家,都為了「英語是否該成為官方語言」而引發全國性的爭議。

▶ 【身處台灣 縱橫美語】

為了嘉惠有心提升英語造詣的讀者,精心編撰本書,內容包羅萬象,從美國大學選課到職場升遷、從生離死別到結婚典禮,從投資理財到電腦科技,從柴米油鹽到政治選舉,逐一呈現美國文化的全面性,讓您身處台灣,卻能接觸到最知性、最感性、最道地的生活英語。

速聽學英語:看電視或是看電影時,你會不會覺得美國人說英語,說得很快,好像口裡含著魯蛋,每一個字都是連成一個字說出來的,實際上,美國人還是一字一字分開說的,只是語調的關係,所以聽起來,好像一句話裡的每個字都是連成一個字。

當你聽得懂美國老師以正常速度念英語時，你的英語聽力和會話，就是到達 A⁺ 英語的階段了。打開耳朵，每天 10 分鐘，本書讓您的英語聽力會話全速起飛。

想要很輕鬆地學會聽說流利的美語，最好的方法是跟著本書由美國專業播音員所錄製的語言 MP3 唸，而且是大聲地唸，聽久了、唸久了這些句子自然成了你的語言。

▶ 【全方位的功能 全方位的讀者】

能聽說流利道地英語，對於在未來想要通過各種升學考、檢定考測驗的學生而言，是致勝關鍵。而對於正在英語系國家求學的留學生來說，更是適應環境，與異國文化深入交流的必要條件。

此外，對於有志從事英語教學工作的老師或是學者們，本書將是您可以善加利用的授課教材。又若您是靠英語吃飯的上班族，本書不但能為你的職場生涯加分，更能為你保住在世界地球村的競爭優勢。倘若您的英語能力已經不錯，但是想要精益求精，增進英語造詣，這本全亞洲最好的英語聽力會話經典，您更是不能錯過！

CHAPTER 1

校園趣談

UNIT 01 | # Who did you get for English?

MP3-02

你的英文老師是誰？

 **Vitamin before class**

新學期開始了，Who did you get for English?（你的英文老師是誰呢？）會不會擔心學期末時英文被當掉呢？與其擔心，還不如好好跟著你的老師學英文吧。讓良好的學習態度成為你的「英文免死金牌」。

➤ 對話一

A： Who did you get for English?

你的英文老師是誰？

B： Dr. Wang.

王博士。

A： Oh she's a great teacher.

喔，她是個好老師耶。

You'll like her.

你會喜歡她的。

B： I know.

　　　我知道。

　　　I dropped by her office to see her this afternoon.

　　　我今天下午去她辦公室看過她了。

▶ 對話二

A： What are your electives?

　　　你選了哪些選修課？

B： Basket-weaving 101, dancing, fencing, and theatre.

　　　籃子編織入門，舞蹈，擊劍，還有戲劇。

A： That is an odd combination.

　　　那是個很奇怪的組合耶。

B： Yes, but that's because I have a wide range of interests.

　　　是呀。那是因為我的興趣很廣泛。

課 後 馬 殺 雞　Massage after class

美國大學的修課選單中，course 101 代表的是基礎入門的課程。一年級的課程代號都是 1 開頭，好比 course 102, course 103, course 104，二年級的課程代號，都是 2 開頭，好比 course 201, course 202, course 203，以此類推，研究所的課程代號，會是幾開頭呢？你猜對了嗎，是 5 開頭唷。

> ## 應用練習

A How many hours are you taking this semester?

B I've got a full-time schedule this fall – twelve hours.

A：這學期你要修多少學分呢？
B：秋季這一學期，我是全職選課－要修十二學分。

A What classes are you taking this summer?

B I'm going to finish up the last of my core requirements in English and Math.

A：這個暑假你要修哪些課？
B：我要修完剩下的英文與數學必修學分。

A I was able to get into Dr. White's Art History class this semester.

B Oh, you're so lucky.
She makes learning really fun.

A：這學期我有機會修懷特博士的藝術史。
B：哇，你真幸運。
　　她確實讓學習變得有趣。

A I have to take this philosophy class, but I don't really like the professor.

B Well, you only have the class two hours a week. Just get the class over with.

A：我得要修這門哲學課，不過我不是很喜歡這個教授。

B：你一星期只需上這門課兩小時。
就把這門課上完吧。

課後馬殺雞 Massage after class

美國大學的課程選修很有彈性，學生可以選擇做一個 full-time student 或 part-time student，一般大學規定要做一個 full-time student，一個學期至少要修 12 個學分，練習會話裡，B 提到他這學期有一個 full-time schedule，並立即加以說明他修了 12 學分的課，換句話說，他這學期是個 full-time student.

在台灣，我們稱九月份開始的學期為第一學期，寒假過後的那個學期為第二學期，在美國，他們稱九月份開始的學期為 fall semester（秋季班），寒假過後的學期為 spring semester（春季班），一般大學暑假也有開課，就是 summer 的課。

單字銀行 Word Bank

Nouns 名詞

extracurricular classes		課外活動
basket-weaving 101		籃子編織入門
fencing	[ˈfɛnsɪŋ]	擊劍
theatre	[ˈθɪətɚ]	戲劇
combination	[ˌkɑmbəˈneʃən]	組合
semester	[səˈmɛstɚ]	學期
schedule	[ˈskɛdʒul]	時間表
core	[kor]	核心；精髓
philosophy	[fəˈlɑsəfɪ]	哲學
professor	[prəˈfɛsɚ]	教授

Adjectives 形容詞

Odd	[ɑd]	古怪，詭異
full-time		全職的；專任的

片語小舖 Phrases Shop

✻ drop by
拜訪

✻ get something over with
完成必須做但不喜歡做的事

UNIT 02 | How do you like your school?

MP3-03

你喜歡你的學校嗎？

課 前 維 他 命 Vitamin before class

在台灣，成績念的好，不僅能夠進名校，而且，台灣的名校都是公立大學，可以幫家長省下很多錢，在美國正好相反，全美排名前二十名的大學，都是私立學校，美國的公立學校最為學生頭痛的一點就是學生人數很多，一個課堂常常是一、兩百個學生，而且也常常遇到沒辦法修到自己想修的課的情形。

➤ 對話一

A : How do you like going to school at such a big university?

去這麼大的大學上課，你喜歡嗎？

B : I love the quality of education I'm getting, but the large classes are a little overwhelming.

我喜歡我要得到的上課品質，不過大課堂有一點讓人有壓力。

A : Yeah, a class filled with 200 students can make you feel a little small.

是呀，兩百多個學生的課堂會讓你覺得自己很渺小。

B : I guess so.

　　我想也是。

　　Maybe I should transfer to a smaller university and see how that suits me.

　　也許我該轉學到較小的大學，看看是否適合我。

➤ **對話二**

A : This semester is really killing me.

　　這學期真是要了我的命。

B : What's the matter?

　　怎麼了？

　　Have your grades fallen?

　　你成績退步了嗎？

A : No, it's just that I'm not used to such a heavy workload.

　　不是，只是我不習慣這麼繁重的課業。

　　I'm taking eighteen hours this semester.

　　這學期我修了十八個學分。

B : Six classes!

　　六堂課！

　　No wonder you're stressed!

　　難怪你壓力這麼大！

➤ 應用練習

A Can you believe how much these textbooks cost?

B They are expensive.
Sometimes it seems like I pay more for the books than the classes.

A：你會相信這些教科書要花這麼多錢嗎？
B：書本很貴的。
　　有時候我覺得，我花在書本上的錢超過我付的學費呢。

A What made you decide to change your major?

B Well, once I began student teaching at the music conservatory, I realized that what I really wanted was to play professionally.

A：是什麼原因讓你決定改變主修？
B：自從我到音樂學院實習教學之後，我就知道自己要的是專業演奏。

A How are your studies going?

B Not bad.
I'm starting to get a real feel for physics so I'm really enjoying the classes now.

A：你的學業如何？
B：不差呀。
　　我開始對物理有感覺，所以現在很愛上物理課。

A It seems like every time I call you, you're studying.
Don't you ever go out?

B I will go out once I graduate in a few weeks.
Until then, I'm a homebody.

A：似乎每次我打電話給你，你都在讀書。
　　你都沒出門過嗎？
B：我幾個星期畢業後，就會出門了。
　　在此之前，我只能當個宅男（女）。

單字銀行 Word Bank

Verbs 動詞

transfer	[ˈtrænsfɚ]	轉學
suit	[sut]	適合
realize	[ˈrɪəˌlaɪz]	明白
graduate	[ˈgrædʒʊˌet]	畢業

Adverbs 副詞

professionally	[prəˈfɛʃənl̩]	專業地

Nouns 名詞

university	[ˌjunəˈvɝsətɪ]	大學
workload	[ˈwɝkˌlod]	工作量
conservatory	[kənˈsɝvəˌtorɪ]	音樂學校
textbook	[ˈtɛkstˌbʊk]	教科書
homebody	[ˈhomˌbɑdɪ]	居家的人

Adjectives 形容詞

heavy	[ˈhɛvɪ]	沈重的
stressed	[strɛst]	有壓力的
Overwhelming	[ˌovɚˈhwɛlmɪŋ]	壓倒性的；讓人喘不過氣的

片語小舖 Phrases Shop

✤ no wonder
難怪

✤ get a real feel for ~
對…有感覺

UNIT 03 | I am getting so burned out on school.

MP3-04

我在學校快要心力交瘁了。

課 前 維 他 命 Vitamin before class

你是個認真向學的學生嗎？你曾因為繁重的課業而心力交瘁嗎？在這個單元裡，我們將要告訴你，如何用英文大聲吶喊，「學業讓我心力交瘁」" I am getting so burned out on school. "

> **對話一**

A : I am getting so burned out on school.

我在學校快要心力交瘁了。

B : Well, Spring Break will do you good then.

春假會讓你好過些的。

A : I can't wait for the break.

我等不及春假了。

I really need some time off from school.

我確實需要離開學校一段時間。

B ： I'll bet that you'll want to get back to your studies after a little vacation.

我敢打賭，休息一陣子你就會想回來上課了。

課 後 馬 殺 雞　Massage after class

美國的春假叫做 Spring Break, 因為 break 有短暫休息的意思。下課了，我們說 Take a break。還記得我們在國中時學過的 breakfast 嗎？ 因為早餐時間，也是一種短暫的休息呢。另外，break 還有『打破』的意思。你們知道「放屁」要怎麼說嗎？ Break wind, 打破周圍的風，也就是「一股毒氣打破四周的空氣。」Got that?（懂了嗎？）

▶ 對話二

A ： How do you think you did on that test?

你覺得你那次考試考的好嗎？

B ： I think I did okay.

我覺得還可以啦。

How about you?

那你呢？

A ： It was pretty easy I thought.

我覺得還滿簡單的。

I'm just glad it's over.

我只是很高興它結束了。

B ： I know.

我知道。

It's nice to get things done.

事情告一段落令人愉快。

> ## 應用練習

A
I'm really worried about my grades.
If I don't maintain a B+ average, I will lose my scholarship.

B
Listen, I know a really good tutor.
Maybe he can help you with your schoolwork.

A：我真的很擔心我的成績。

如果我的平均沒有維持在 B+，我就會失去獎學金了。

B：聽好，我知道一個很棒的家教。

也許他能幫助你的課業。

A
Are you going to go to the university ball this Friday?

B
I want to but I can't.
I've got an exam the following morning I need to study for.

A：這週五你要去參加大學舞會嗎？

B：我想去，但去不了。
我需要準備隔天早上的考試。

A Did you hear about the science seminar coming to campus this Tuesday?

B Yeah, I did.
I'm really excited about the chaos theory lecture by Dr. Smith.

A：你有聽說這週二要在本校舉行的科學研究會嗎？

B：有呀。
我對史密斯博士的混沌理論演講感到興奮不已。

A I'm thinking about running for student government.
What do you think?

B I think you'd make a great student senator.
Students would definitely vote for you.

A：我正在考慮參選學生會。
你認為如何？

B：我想你會是一個很棒的學生議員。
學生們一定會投票給你的。

單字銀行 Word Bank

Verbs 動詞

bet	[bɛt]	打賭
maintain	[men'ten]	維持，保持

Adverbs 副詞

| definitely | ['dɛfənɪtlɪ] | 明確地；一定是… |

Nouns 名詞

Spring Break		春假
break	[brek]	休息
tutor	['tjutɚ]	家教
the science seminar		科學研討會
campus	['kæmpəs]	校園
the chaos theory		混沌理論
lecture	['lɛktʃɚ]	演講，講課內容
student government		學生會
student senator		學生議員
average	['ævərɪdʒ]	平均
scholarship	['skɑlɚˌʃɪp]	獎學金

片語小舖 Phrases Shop

❋ **be burned out**
  心力交瘁

Smart 舒壓建議

一、釋放情緒：生活的週遭有太多影響情緒的因子，包括太
　　過在乎、太在意得失等，如果能用更寬廣的視野去解讀
　　世事，就比較容易釋放情緒，跳脫被情緒綑綁的束縛。

二、平衡呼吸頻率：呼吸是我們最自然的本能。能夠利用簡
　　單而正確的呼吸，規律我們生理的頻率，就容易得到自
　　我和外在的平衡。

三、休息與睡眠：在長期接收壓力累積的情況中，充足的休
　　息和睡眠對放鬆是極為重要的。

四、緩和人際關係：人與人之間的互動，是最纖細且不可完
　　全理解的關係，但如果能懷抱著一種和平的心境，自然
　　可以迎刃而解生活上瑣碎複雜的人際關係。

五、沉澱心靈：多給自己一些正面思考的方向，讓心靈跳脫
　　制式的生活模式，讓情緒得以紓緩，壓力自然就消失無
　　蹤了。

UNIT 04 | What clubs should I join?

我應該加入哪一個社團？

課前維他命 Vitamin before class

你在學校的時候，有參與過 student newspaper（學生報）的編輯工作嗎？在美國，如果 student newspaper 報導學生壓力過大，學校的 Student Health Center（學生健康中心）還會提供廉價的馬殺雞呢！至於有多廉價，往下看就知道。

▶ 對話一

A : My friend is trying to get me to join his fraternity.
我的朋友在説服我參加他的兄弟會。

B : It doesn't sound like you want to join.
聽起來你不是很想參加。

A : I can't really decide.
我實在無法做決定。

It sounds like fun, and he's been my friend for a long time.

（兄弟會）聽起來很有趣，而且他是老朋友了。

But I'd like to do something different.

不過我想做點不一樣的事情。

B : The soccer team is different, and I know they are having tryouts this Saturday.

足球隊很不一樣，而且我知道他們這週六將有選拔賽。

A : Yeah, soccer is definitely something I like.

是呀，我確實喜歡足球。

▶ 對話二

A : Did you hear about the health seminar the Student Health Center is holding?

你有聽說學生健康中心正要舉行的健康研討會嗎？

B : No, what's going on?

沒有耶，是怎麼回事？

A : In response to the reports of student stress, they will offer $5 full body massages all day tomorrow.

為了回應學生的壓力報導，明天一整天他們將提供五塊錢的全身馬殺雞。

B : You're kidding!

你在開玩笑吧！

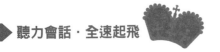

That's so cheap!

這麼便宜！

And I need one with my stiff neck.

我僵硬的脖子需要按摩一下。

> **應用練習**

A I think I would feel more at home here if I could be a part of a group.

B Why don't you come with me to the philosophy club meeting tonight?
It might be something you'd enjoy.

A：如果我能成為一個團體裡的一份子，我在這裡會比較
有歸屬感。

B：今晚你何不跟我去哲學社的聚會？
你可能會喜歡唷。

A You know, the student newspaper has really improved since last semester.

B Oh yeah, the quality of the stories is so much better than what it used to be.

A：你知道的，從上學期起，學生報真的進步了。

B：喔是呀，故事的品質比起過去真是好太多了。

A Have you decided to live on or off campus?

B I chose to live in the dorms on campus so I could be near everything that was going on.

A：你已決定好要住校內或是校外了嗎？

B：我選擇住在學校宿舍好貼近任何發生的事情。

課後馬殺雞 Massage after class

你知道美國大學的「學生福利社」要怎麼說嗎？

答案是：Student Union 除了販賣點心飲料，Student Union 還會定期舉辦電影欣賞會等。至於吃正餐的地方，才叫做 cafeteria。

單字銀行 Word Bank

Verbs 動詞

decide	[dɪˈsaɪd]	決定
offer	[ˈɔfɚ]	提供
improve	[ɪmˈpruv]	進步

Nouns 名詞

fraternity	[frəˈtɝnətɪ]	兄弟會
tryout	[ˈtraɪˌaʊt]	選拔會
Soccer	[ˈsakɚ]	足球
the Student Health Center		學生健康中心
report	[rɪˈport]	報導
stress	[strɛs]	壓力
full body massage		全身馬殺雞
group	[grup]	團體
the student newspaper		學生報
quality	[ˈkwɑlətɪ]	品質
dorms	[dɔrm]	宿舍（dormitory 的簡稱）

Adjectives 形容詞

| cheap | [tʃip] | 便宜的 |
| stiff | [stɪf] | 僵硬的 |

片語小舖 Phrases Shop

❋ in response to
為了回應⋯

MEMO

UNIT
05

How are you doing at school?

你的課業好嗎？

課前維他命 **Vitamin before class**

你曾有過科目被當的經驗嗎？還是都能過關斬將，all pass 呢？如果你是老師，你會不會很想「當人」呢？說真的，對於一個仁慈的老師來說，要「當人」也是一件痛苦的事情呀。其實，要避免「被當」也很簡單，就 study harder 吧。

➤ 對話一

A： At first I thought a self-paced class would be so easy.

一開始我以為自我進度的課程是很簡單的。

But it's my most difficult class.

不過這是我最感到困難的課了。

B： I tried a self-paced class a year ago, and I failed it. Never again.

一年前我上過一門自我進度的課，被當了。 不想再試了。

A ： Why did you fail?

你為何被當呢？

B ： I'm just not the kind of person that learns well without class time.

我不是那種不上課也能學得好的人。

If I'm on my own, I don't even think about studying.

如果只靠自己，我根本不想讀。

I just got behind.

我自然落後了。

➤ 對話二

A ： Can you believe the semester is almost over?

你相信嗎？這學期幾乎要結束了。

B ： It does seem like this spring has just flown by.

似乎春季這學期就這樣過去了。

A ： What will you do over the summer?

今年夏天你打算做什麼？

B ： After I graduate, I'm going to Europe for a month.

畢業後，我要去歐洲一個月。

> **應用練習**

A I have changed my major so many times that I wonder if I'll ever get out of college.

B Stop making it so difficult on yourself, stay with a subject you like.

A：我的主修已經更改很多次了，我懷疑自己是否能畢的了業。

B：別再讓自己的日子難過了，擇定一個你喜歡的科系吧。

A I got an A on my psychology test!

B Really? Everyone I know didn't do too well – myself included.

A：我的心理學考試拿了 A!

B：真的嗎？ 我所認識的人都沒考好，包括我自己。

A I decided to get you another backpack for your birthday.

B Thanks! My other one is practically falling apart.

A：我決定再買個背包給你，當作你的生日禮物。

B：謝謝！我的另個背包已經快破了。

A The insurance provided by the school really helps international students.

B How so?

A When I first got here, I was sick as a dog. The school insurance helped pay my medical bills.

A：學校的保險確實幫助了國際學生。

B：怎麼講呢？

A：我剛到這裡時像個病狗一樣。
　　學校的保險幫我支付了醫療費用。

課後馬殺雞 Massage after class

backpack 除了當「背包」，解釋，也可作為「自助旅行」之意，
那就是把需要的東西放在一個背包裡，背著就旅行去了。
例句：I want to backpack around America this summer.
這個暑假我想去美國自助旅行。

單字銀行 Word Bank

Verbs 動詞

Fail	[fel]	科目被當，不及格
Change	[tʃendʒ]	改變
Wonder	[ˈwʌndɚ]	懷疑；想知道…
Include	[ɪnˈklud]	包含
Provide	[prəˈvaɪd]	提供

Adverbs 副詞

practically	[ˈpræktɪklɪ]	實際地；事實上

Nouns 名詞

self-paced class		自我進度的課程
subject	[ˈsʌbdʒɪkt]	科目
insurance	[ɪnˈʃurəns]	保險
backpack	[ˈbækˌpæk]	背包

Adjectives 形容詞

difficult	[ˈdɪfəˌkəlt]	困難的
medical	[ˈmɛdɪkl̩]	醫學的

片語小舖 Phrases Shop

❋ **get behind**
落後

❋ **fly by**
時間飛逝

❋ **get out of college**
離開大學（大學畢業）

❋ **fall apart**
脫落，變成碎片

MEMO

CHAPTER 2

社交場合

UNIT 06 | What a beautiful wedding!

好一場漂亮的婚禮！

MP3-07

Vitamin before class

Here comes the bride!（新娘來了！）

還記得『落跑新娘』（Runway Bride) 這部電影嗎，女主角茱利亞羅伯茲總共在婚禮中落跑了三次！之後的篇章，我們會提到 getaway car, 讀者們不妨先猜猜看，getaway car 是什麼樣的車子，是否有其特殊的功能呢？

> **對話一**

A ： What a beautiful day for an outdoor wedding!

對一場戶外婚禮而言，今天是多麼美麗的日子呀。

B ： Yes, the weather is lovely.

是呀，天氣真好。

I can't wait to see her in her wedding dress.

我等不及要看她穿上結婚禮服了。

A ： It's really gorgeous.

那禮服真的很華麗。

She showed me the other day.

前幾天她展示給我看了。

B : Oh, stand up! Here comes the bride!

喔，起立！新娘來了！

➤ 對話二

A : Congratulations, Tom! What an exciting day for you!

恭喜呀湯姆！對你來說這是多麼讓人興奮的一天呀！

B : I know! I'm still nervous.

我知道！我還是很緊張。

Have you had a good time?

你玩的盡興嗎？

A : I'm having a great time.

我玩得很開心呢，

Thank you for inviting me.

謝謝你邀請我來。

B : Thanks for coming, Steve.

謝謝你的光臨，史提夫。

I'm glad you could make it.

我很高興你能來。

> **應用練習**

A Do you know the bride or groom?

B The groom was an old college buddy of mine.

A：你認識新娘或是新郎嗎？
B：新郎是我的大學死黨之一。

A What a wedding cake!
It must have ten tiers!

B If you think that's impressive, look at that beautiful groom's cake.

A：這就是婚禮蛋糕！
它應該有十層。
B：如果你覺得它讓你印象深刻，看看那個美麗的新郎蛋糕吧。

A Hello! You look nice.
Are you ready to be a bridesmaid?

B No sweat. I've done this many times.
You know what they say – always a bridesmaid, never a bride!

A：哈囉！你看起來很不錯呢。
準備好要當伴娘了嗎？

B：那沒什麼，我已經當過很多次了。
你知道的，人們都說：老是當伴娘的人，當不了新娘！

A Hey John! We're going to decorate the getaway car.
Want to come?

B Yeah, that would be fun.
I think Tom has some shaving cream we could use.

A：嘿，約翰！我們要去裝飾禮車了。
想過來嗎？

B：好呀，應該滿有趣的。
我想我們可以用湯姆的刮鬍膏。

課後馬殺雞 Massage after class

相信很多人都參加過『喜宴』（wedding feast）吧？美國的婚禮
文化有別於台灣。結婚這檔事，由女方主辦。換句話說，新娘
的爸爸要『破費』啦。

單字銀行 Word Bank

Verbs 動詞

decorate	[ˈdɛkəˌret]	裝飾

Nouns 名詞

wedding	[ˈwɛdɪŋ]	結婚典禮
wedding dress		結婚禮服
congratulation	[kənˌɡrætʃəˈleʃən]	恭喜
bride	[braɪd]	新娘
groom	[grum]	新郎
buddy	[ˈbʌdɪ]	死黨，夥伴
tier	[tɪr]	層數
bridesmaid	[ˈbraɪdzˌmed]	伴娘
getaway	[ˈɡɛtəˌwe]	逃亡
getaway car		禮車（ 在其他場合，當『逃亡車』解釋)
shaving cream		刮鬍膏

Adjectives　形容詞

outdoor	['aʊt,dor]	戶外的
lovely	['lʌvlɪ]	美好的
gorgeous	['gɔrdʒəs]	華麗的
nervous	['nɝvəs]	緊張的
impressive	[ɪm'prɛsɪv]	令人印象深刻

MEMO

UNIT 07 | Happy birthday!
祝你生日快樂！

課前維他命 Vitamin before class

你喜歡幫別人慶生嗎？有機會的話，throw me a surprise party（給我一個驚喜派對）吧！其實，每過一個生日，意味著又老了一歲，真難想像有一天，別人在我的慶生會上問我：How does it feel to be 100?（一百歲是什麼感覺？），我希望我還能高高興興的接受別人慶生。

> ### 對話一

A： Hey, happy birthday!
　　嘿，生日快樂！

How does it feel to be 23?
　　二十三歲是什麼感覺？

B： I don't feel any different actually.
　　說真的我不覺得有何不同耶。

Come on in.
　　進來吧

A ： Wow, this place looks great, and the food smells wonderful!

哇，這地方看起來很棒，而且食物聞起來很香！

B ： Take your coats off and make yourselves at home.

把你的外套脫下，把這裡當作你家吧。

The gang's all here.

死黨們都在這。

▶ **對話二**

A ： Surprise! Happy birthday!

給你一個驚喜！ 生日快樂呀！

B ： I can't believe you guys threw me a surprise party.

真不敢相信你們這群人給我來個驚喜派對。

A ： You didn't suspect anything?

你都沒察覺到任何不對勁嗎？

B ： I honestly had no idea.

我真的什麼都不知道。

You guys did a pretty good job of keeping the secret.

你們這些人真會保密。

> **應用練習**

A This is a great birthday.
Everyone I know is here.

B Well, we thought you deserved it.

A：這是個很棒的生日。
我所認識的每個人都在這裡。
B：嗯，我們認為這是你該得的。

A I'm glad we decided to just have a small gathering of people for my birthday.
I don't really like big parties.

B I agree. It's always nice to have a few friends over for coffee and cake.

A：我很高興，我們只讓一小群人來幫我慶生。
我不是很喜歡大派對。
B：我同意。能夠邀一些朋友來享用咖啡與蛋糕總是美事。

A So do you know the birthday boy?

B No, I know his sister.
I came here with her.

A：那你認識壽星嗎？

B：不，我認識他姊姊。

我跟她一起來的。

A This cake is delicious!
Where did you get it?

B I made it myself, silly!

A：這蛋糕真美味！

你在哪裡買的？

B：我自己做的啦，傻瓜！

課後馬殺雞 Massage after class

在這裡，要告訴讀者一個 silly 這個英文單字的小故事。話說台灣扁政府打算在 2004 年的總統大選當日舉辦全民公投。對於此事，美國外交首長淡淡地說了一句 " Silly." 當時全國各報通通把這句話解讀為『愚蠢』，其實，這句話的意思是『無聊』『沒必要嘛！』的意思。光是 "silly" 就有好幾種解讀，所以我們怎能輕忽語言的力量呢。

單字銀行 Word Bank

Nouns 名詞

birthday boy		壽星
silly	['sɪlɪ]	傻瓜

片語小舖 Phrases Shop

※ make oneself at home
  當作是在自己的家一樣（讓自己自在一點）

UNIT 08 | Are you having a good time?

MP3-09

你玩得愉快嗎？

課前維他命 Vitamin before class

你有辦過派對的經驗嗎？如果看到邀請名單上的人光臨，你一定會很興奮地說：I'm glad you could make it！（我好高興你能來！）

make it，在這裡指的是能夠排除萬難，配合別人的時間去參與某件事。

> **對話一**

A ： Hey! I'm glad you could make it!

嘿！我好高興你能來！

B ： How's it going, Terry?

一切都順利嗎，泰瑞？

Look like this party is swinging.

這派對看起來變熱鬧的。

A : Oh yeah, we've got a lot of people here tonight.
喔是呀，今晚來了很多人。

Can I get you a drink?
要我幫你拿杯飲料嗎？

B : I'd love one, thanks.
我想要一杯，謝謝。

> ➤ **對話二**

A : You look like you're having a good time, Sam.
你看起來玩得很盡興耶，山姆。

B : I am. I haven't been to a party in ages.
是呀。我已經很多年沒參加派對了。

A : Do you want to dance?
你想跳舞嗎？

B : Yes, I'd love to.
好呀，我很樂意。

➤ 應用練習

A Hey you! How's it going?

B Gary! It's so nice to see you!
Isn't this a great party?

A：嘿，你這傢伙！ 近來一切可好？
B：蓋瑞！能見到你真是棒！
這派對很棒吧？

A Why such a glum face at a party?

B Oh, I'm just a little down because my girlfriend
broke up with me last night.

A：為何在派對裡悶悶不樂呢？
B：喔，我只是心情有一點不好，因為昨晚我跟女友吹了。

A If we don't keep it down, my neighbors are
going to call the cops.

B Okay, I'll stop the music and tell everybody to
keep it down.

A：如果我們不小聲一點，我的鄰居會打電話叫警察的。
B：好吧，我會把音樂關掉並且告訴每個人把音量放低。

A Who is this party for?

B We're having a party for Mary.
She got promoted.

A：這派對是為誰開的？

B：我們正在幫瑪麗舉行派對。
　　她獲得升遷。

課後馬殺雞 Massage after class

當 A 先生與 B 小姐之間感情決裂而宣告分手時，我們可以說：
They broke up.（他們吹了）另外，在美國口語裡，警察叫做
cop, 而非 police。

單字銀行 Word Bank

Nouns 名詞

age	[edʒ]	年
cop	[kɑp]	警察

Adjectives 形容詞

swinging	['swɪŋɪŋ]	（宴會）人很多而且大家玩得很愉快
glum	[glʌm]	鬱鬱寡歡的

片語小舖 Phrases Shop

❀ break up with someone
跟某人分手

MP3-10

UNIT 09 | Let's have a picnic.

我們去野餐吧。

課前維他命 Vitamin before class

你同意 food always seems to taste better out of doors（在戶外，食物嚐起來總是比較可口）嗎？若是如此，你一定要好好利用 pretty days（好天氣）去 picnic（野餐）。

> **對話一**

A : Would you like some apple pie?
你想要來點蘋果派嗎？

I made it myself.
我自己做的唷。

B : Yes, I love apple pie.
好呀，我喜歡吃蘋果派。

This picnic was a really nice idea.
這次野餐真是個好主意。

A ： Well, it's such a pretty day and the kids really enjoy playing outside.

嗯，這是個美好的一天，孩子們在外頭也玩得很樂。

B ： I saw them playing games with their grandfather earlier.

之前我還看到他們跟他們的祖父一起玩遊戲。

➤ 對話二

A ： John, could you grab some blankets?

約翰，你能弄一些毯子來嗎？

B ： Sure. Where are we going to picnic?

當然可以。 我們要去哪裡野餐？

A ： I thought maybe we'd check out that picnic area by the lake.

我想我們可能會在湖邊野餐。

B ： Great idea.

好主意。

Hey! We'd better bring some insect repellent.

嘿！我們最好帶一點驅蟲劑。

➤ 應用練習

A I haven't picnicked since I was a kid.

B I love eating outside on a pretty day.
Food always seems to taste better out of doors.

A：長大以後，我就沒有野餐過。
B：我喜歡在好日子時出外野餐。
在戶外，食物嚐起來總是比較可口。

A This barbecue is delicious.
Could I have some more beans?

B Sure. Most people like to make sandwiches for a picnic, but I like some good hot food.

A：這烤肉真是美味。
我能再吃點豆子嗎？
B：當然。大部分的人喜歡做三明治去野餐，不過我喜歡熱騰騰的食物。

A We've got watermelon on the other picnic table if anybody wants some.

B Mmmm. Watermelon is great after a picnic.

A：我們把西瓜放在另一個野餐桌，想取用的人請便。

B：嗯。野餐後有西瓜吃是很讚的。

A Summertime was made for picnics.

B Yeah, I never feel like it's summer until I've had a picnic.

A：夏天是野餐的好時機。

B：是呀，直到我野餐後才覺得夏天來了。

課後馬殺雞 Massage after class

求學過程中，總是會有幾個老師讓人印象深刻（impressive）。
在美國時，我那七十幾歲的指導教授曾帶幾個學生去紐約州的
Bear MT.（大熊山）野餐。

Bear MT. 隸屬紐約州立公園，景色非常優美。我在那裡沒有看
到任何『熊跡』，反倒在山頭驚見一頭美麗的野鹿（deer）。那
次野餐，師母準備了壽司，辣味雞翅（spicy wings），以及洋芋
（potato）。為了感謝教授與師母的招待，我們就在附近的禮品
店（gift shop）合買了一個玻璃鹿畫送給他們。

單字銀行 Word Bank

Nouns 名詞

barbecue	['barbɪkju]	烤肉
sandwich	['sændwɪtʃ]	三明治
watermelon	['wɔtɚ,mɛlən]	西瓜
taste	[test]	味道；體驗；品嚐（註：taste 亦可作動詞用）

MEMO

UNIT 10 | We're throwing a farewell party for John.

MP3-11

我們要為約翰舉辦一個歡送會。

課 前 維 他 命 Vitamin before class

人生無不散的宴席。『送別會』(farewell party; going away party) 代表著一種結束，也意味著另一個開始。但如果是知心好友，說出一句窩心的 keep in touch（保持聯絡），就勝過千言萬語了。

➤ 對話一

A : Here's to Charlie!

　　我來敬查里一杯。

　　May he enjoy his new job and home in Pittsburgh!

　　祝他樂在新工作與匹茲堡的生活。

B : Thanks, Tom.

　　謝謝你呀湯姆。

　　I really appreciate you guys going through all of this trouble to give me a going away party.

　　我真的很感謝你們不計辛苦的為我辦一場送別會。

A : Are you kidding?

你在開什麼玩笑？

It was no trouble.

沒什麼麻煩的。

You're a good friend.

你是個好朋友。

We wanted to send you off in style.

我們想為你辦個有品味的送行。

B : Well, you certainly did a good job of that.

嗯，你們真的做的很棒。

This has been quite a party.

這是一個相當棒的派對。

> ## 對話二

A : We're really going to miss you, Mary.

我們會很想你的，瑪麗。

B : I'll only be gone for six months.

我只是去六個月而已。

I'll be back before you know it.

在你們還沒察覺時間已到之時，我就回來了。

A : I'm so jealous of your going to Spain to study flamenco.

我真羨慕你去西班牙學佛朗明哥舞。

B ： It's something I've always wanted to do.

這是我一直想做的事。

Now that I'm retired, I've got the time.

現在我退休了，有時間了。

➤ 應用練習

A
This farewell party has made me so sad.
I don't want to leave now.

B
You'll get over that once you settle into your new place.
Just keep in touch.

A：這場送別會讓我好傷感。
現在我不想離開了。

B：一旦你在新地方安定好後，你會恢復心情的。
就繼續保持聯絡吧。

A
Now promise to write often.
And as soon as I get a chance I'll come visit.

B
I will. And thank you for putting together this farewell party.
It was really thoughtful of you.

A：答應我要常通信唷。
　　我一有機會，就會來探望你的。
B：我會的。也謝謝你籌辦這場送別會。
　　你真體貼。

A I can't tell you how much this farewell party means to me.
You guys are truly good friends.

B Well, we love you, Susan.
You just take care of yourself.

A：我無法向你形容這場送別會對我的意義有多大。
　　你們真是一群好朋友。
B：嗯，我們很愛你的，蘇珊。
　　你要好好保重。

A I think Joan is really touched that we threw this going away party for her.

B I know I would be.
It's nice to know that you'll be missed.

A：我想，瓊恩真的很感動我們為她辦了這場送別會。
B：若是我，我也會感動的。
　　知道自己將被懷念是值得高興的。

課後馬殺雞 Massage after class

1. 海明威的小說『戰地春夢』，英文叫做 A farewell to Arms。
2. throw, 原本是拋、丟的意思。在美國口語裡，幫別人『辦』
   派對，也可以用 throw 這個動詞。

單字銀行 Word Bank

Verbs 動詞

retire	[rɪˈtaɪr]	退休
appreciate	[əˈpriʃɪˌet]	感謝；欣賞

Adverbs 副詞

certainly	[ˈsɝtənlɪ]	確實，真的

Nouns 名詞

Pittsburgh	[ˈpɪtsbɝg]	匹茲堡
flamenco	[flɑˈmɛŋko]	佛朗明哥舞
style	[staɪl]	風格

Adjectives 形容詞

jealous	[ˈdʒɛləs]	羨慕，嫉妒

片語小舖 Phrases Shop

❋ go through
經歷

❋ send off
送行

MEMO

MP3-12

UNIT
11
What are you getting Mary for her wedding?

你要送瑪麗什麼結婚禮物？

課 前 維 他 命 Vitamin before class

你知道什麼是 baby shower 嗎？在台灣，新生兒滿月時，小嬰兒的爹地媽咪都會送蛋糕或油飯給親朋好友。但是在美國，情勢可不同啦。新生兒的父母親藉由 baby shower, 可以收到朋友們給小嬰兒的禮物與關心唷。

▶ 對話一

A : I love baby showers.

> 我喜歡新生兒的送禮派對。

It makes me want to have one of my own.

> 這讓我想要生個孩子。

B : Well, the showers certainly do help a new mom get on her feet.

> 嗯，送禮派對確實能幫助一個新媽媽站穩腳步。

A : Oh I can imagine.

喔，這我能想像。

With all of the stuff the little guy needs, it's nice to have some help.

小傢伙需要那麼多東西，能夠得到一點幫助是好的。

B : Yes it is.

確實如此。

I've had three and the financial burden a shower relieves is amazing.

我有三個小孩，送禮派對對財物上負擔的減輕實在驚人。

➤ 對話二

A : This is a pretty formal wedding shower.

這是一個非常正式的婚禮送禮派對。

B : Yeah, I don't think I've ever been to one where speeches were given.

是呀，我不曾參加過有演講的送禮派對。

A : I think when I get married, I'm going to insist that the shower be a casual affair.

等我結婚時，我會堅持要辦個輕鬆的送禮派對。

B : Me too. Too much formality makes me uncomfortable.

我也是。太正式會讓我感到不自在。

➤ 應用練習

A Where should I put the wedding gift?

B There's a table in the dining room for all of the gifts.

A：我應該把送給新人的禮物放在哪裡？
B：在餐廳裡有一張禮品置物桌。

A Look at all these adorable baby clothes!
They're so small.

B I love the little dresses.
So tiny! So cute!

A：看看這些美麗的嬰兒服！
它們好小唷。
B：我喜歡這些小洋裝。
好迷你！好可愛！

A These petit fours are so neat!
Where did you get them?

B The bakery down the road makes them.

A：這些小餅乾好精緻！
　　妳在哪裡買的？
B：路底的那家糕餅店賣的。

課後馬殺雞　Massage after class

大家學過 shower 是洗淋浴的意思，那麼什麼是 wedding shower 和 baby shower 呢？那就是大夥兒送新娘子或是準媽媽很多的禮物，好像用禮物來把新娘子或準媽媽 shower（淋的一身都是）一樣。wedding shower 和 baby shower 都是由新娘子和準媽媽的好友來舉辦，只准女性參加，在這個宴會上，大家帶來給新娘子或準媽媽的禮物，一方面好友慶祝她們要結婚或是要當媽媽了，一方面也帶給一個新家庭，或是新添小寶寶的準媽媽一些必備的東西，減輕她們經濟上的負擔。

單字銀行 Word Bank

Verbs 動詞

relieve	[rɪˈliv]	減輕；解除

Nouns 名詞

shower	[ˈʃaʊɚ]	送禮派對
burden	[ˈbɝdn̩]	負擔

formality	[fɔr'mælətɪ]	正式
dining room		餐廳
tradition	[trə'dɪʃən]	傳統
petit four		小蛋糕

Adjectives 形容詞

financial	[faɪ'nænʃəl]	財務的
amazing	[ə'mezɪŋ]	驚人的
casual	['kæʒʊəl]	隨意的
adorable	[ə'dorəbl̩]	可愛的
tiny	['taɪnɪ]	極小的
neat	[nit]	精緻

片語小舖 Phrases Shop

❋ get on one's feet
上軌道；自立

UNIT 12 | Let's get together sometime.

我們有時間可以聚一聚。

課前維他命 Vitamin before class

東方人見面，總會寒暄幾句，好比問對方一聲『吃飽沒？』。西方人見到老友則說：How's it going?（近來如何？）或是 What's up?（最近還好吧？）若是見到久未謀面的朋友，則說：Long time no see.（好久不見）。

➤ 對話一

A ： Judy! Hi. Long time no see.

朱蒂！嗨。好久沒見你了。

How's it going?

一切都好嗎？

B ： It's going good, Sue.

一切都好，蘇。

You know, I was going to call you last night to see if you could come over to the house sometime.

你知道嗎，昨晚我本想打電話邀你找個時間來我家。

A ： Well, I can't this week.

嗯，我這禮拜不行。

I'm swamped with work.

我有很多工作要做。

How about next week?

下禮拜如何？

B ： That would be great! Friday then?

那很好！週五如何？

A ： Friday it is. See you then!

就週五吧。到時候見！

B ： Bye Sue.

再見了，蘇。

▶ 對話二

A ： Bobby, I need to talk to you.

巴比，我需要跟你談談。

Do you think we could get together for lunch or something?

你認為我們能一起吃個午餐或什麼之類的嗎？

B ： Sure Tim. What are you doing tomorrow?

當然可以呀，提姆。你明天有什麼要忙的嗎？

A ： I'm free tomorrow.

我整個明天都有空。

. . . .

B ： Well then, let's do lunch tomorrow.

那好，我們明天一起共進午餐吧。

. . . .

> ## ➤ 應用練習

A Mary, could you get together with me to discuss the Byron case sometime soon?

B Absolutely. Let's have coffee tomorrow morning.
I'll catch you up then.

A：瑪麗，你能盡快找個時間跟我討論拜倫的案子嗎？

B：那當然。我們明早去喝個咖啡吧。

到時，我再告訴你我們的進展如何。

A Robert! Hey I can't make 1:00 with you today. Can we meet some other time?

B Sure. Drop by my office before you leave.

A：羅伯！嘿，我今天一點無法跟你見面。
我們能改個時間見面嗎？

B：當然。在你離開之前到我的辦公室來吧。

A Why don't you join us for drinks?
We're meeting at Toscano's at 5:00.

B Okay, I'll be there.

A：為何不加入我們一起喝酒呢？
五點時我們將在托斯卡諾會面。

B：好的，我會到。

A Would it possible for you to set aside some time
for me to discuss my paper?

B Yes, it would. How does 3:30 tomorrow sound?

A：你能抽個空來跟我討論我的報告嗎？

B：可以呀。明天三點半如何？

課 後 馬 殺 雞 Massage after class

美國口語中，do 的妙用無窮。吃午餐，也可以說 do lunch。
如果你打算在週末大量閱讀，也可以說成：I will do a lot of
reading this weekend.

單字銀行 Word Bank

Verbs 動詞

discuss	[dɪˈskʌs]	討論

片語小舖 Phrases Shop

❀ be swamped with
忙得不可開交

❀ catch up
趕上

CHAPTER 3

請假

UNIT 13 | I'm sick.

我病了。

課前維他命 Vitamin before class

你曾在上班期間請過病假（sick leave) 嗎？如果你擔心工作進度而不好意思請假，此時，若有好心的同事雪中送炭來一句：We'll cover for you.（我們會幫你打理的），那該有多好呀。

> **對話一**

A : Hello Mr. Lee?
　　　哈囉，李先生？

　　　This is Jonh Winters.
　　　我是約翰溫特斯。

　　　I'm afraid I won't be able to make it to work this week.
　　　這禮拜我恐怕不能上班。

B : What's the problem, John?
　　　有什麼問題嗎，約翰？

A : The doctor said that I have a virus, and I need to stay at home for at least a week.

　　醫生說我感染了病毒，所以我必須待在家裡至少一個禮拜。

B : I'm sorry to hear that, John.

　　我很遺憾聽到這個消息，約翰。

　　Are you taking any medicine?

　　你有吃藥嗎？

A : Yes, I have a prescription.

　　有呀，我有處方。

　　I'm awfully sorry about this.

　　對於這件事我感到相當抱歉。

B : Don't worry about it.

　　別擔心。

　　You just get well.

　　你只管把病養好。

　　Let us know how you're doing.

　　讓我們瞭解你的情況。

➤ 對話二

A : What's the matter, John?

　　　怎麼啦，約翰？

　　　You sound awful.

　　　你聲音聽起來很糟糕。

B : I feel awful.

　　　我覺得很不舒服。

　　　I've got the flu.

　　　我感冒了。

A : Oh no. I guess you won't be coming to work for a while then.

　　　喔不。我猜你有陣子不能來上班了。

B : I'm afraid so.

　　　恐怕是這樣。

　　　Can Mary cover for me?

　　　瑪麗能幫我打理嗎？

A : I don't think she'll have a problem.

　　　我想她應該沒問題吧。

　　　You take care of yourself.

　　　你好好保重身體。

➤ 應用練習

A Hello Susan.
I'm sorry, but I can't come in for work today.
I'm sick.

B Okay Tim, we'll cover for you.
Stay in bed and get well.

A：哈囉，蘇珊。
很抱歉我今天不能來上班。
我生病了。

B：沒關係的提姆，我們會幫你打理一切。
待在床上等著康復吧。

A You don't look so well, Gina.
Maybe you should take the day off.

B Thanks, I think I will.
I don't feel well at all.

A：你看起來不太好耶，吉娜。
也許你應該請假一天。

B：謝謝，我會的。
我很不舒服。

A John, would it be all right if I took a few days off?
I don't feel so good.

B That's fine, Mary.
I just want you well for next week's board meeting.

A：約翰，我可以請個幾天假嗎？
我覺得不太舒服。

B：好的，瑪麗。
我只希望下禮拜的董事會議你能來。

A I think I'm sick, Ray.

B You look sick.
Yep, you're burning up.
Take the day off and call me tomorrow if you still feel bad.

A：我想我生病了，瑞。

B：你看起來不太好。
是呀，你在發燒。
請個假吧。若還是不舒服，明天打個電話給我。

 課後馬殺雞 Massage after class

上班時若遇到病情嚴重的情況，請個假仍是必要的。之前 SARS 來勢洶洶，機關學校為了預防疫情擴散，個個上緊發條，只要有人當日早上體溫超過攝氏 37.5 度，就要 take a day off，乖乖留在家裡了。

單字銀行 Word Bank

Nouns 名詞

virus	['vaɪrəs]	病毒
flu	[flu]	流行性感冒 （註：禽流感 avainflu）
prescription	[prɪ'skrɪpʃən]	處方
board meeting		董事會

Adjectives 形容詞

awful	['ɔfʊl]	可怕的

片語小舖 Phrases Shop

❋ get well
  康復

❋ burn up
  燒壞

❋ take a (the) day off
  請假

————小測驗 Check List————

病毒 v_____s
流行性感冒 f___
處方 p_____n
board meeting _____

UNIT 14 | I'm taking some days off.

MP3-15

我要請幾天假。

課前維他命 Vitamin before class

本單元裡的主角們，同是天涯淪落人，個個都為了『家務事』而請假。有人為了祖母要搬到 nursing home（養老院）而請假，有人則為了曉家的兒子請假，anyway，一起來看看其他人的請假理由是什麼吧。

➤ 對話一

A ： Ron, I'm going to need some time off from work.

容，我要向公司請幾天假。

B ： What's the matter, Joann?

發生什麼事了，瓊安？

A ： My mother has to have some surgery and I would like to be there with her.

我母親要動一些手術，我想待在她身邊陪著她。

B : Of course, I understand.

那當然的。我能理解。

Take care of your mother.

好好照顧你母親。

We'll keep in touch through your cell phone.

用手機跟我保持聯絡。

I hope she pulls through this.

我希望她能渡過一切。

A : So do I. Thanks.

我也是，謝謝你。

> ## 對話二

A : Mary, I'd like to take a few days off to take care of some family problems.

瑪麗，我想請幾天假去處理一些家務事。

B : Okay. How much time do you need?

好的。你需要多少時間？

A : I'm not sure.

我不確定。

My son is going through a rough time, and I need to be there for him.

我的兒子正面臨難關，我需要陪著他。

B : Of course.

　　　那當然。

　　　Tell you what: you take this week off. After that, we'll play it by ear. Okay?

　　　聽我說，就請這禮拜吧。之後，我們再見機行事吧，如何？

A : Okay, thank you.

　　　好的，謝謝你。

 **Massage after class**

請一天假，take a day off。請幾天假，take a few days off，或是 take a couple of days off。

見機行事，叫做 play it by ear。所謂眼觀四面，耳聽八方，耳朵（ear）似乎比眼睛更能洞察情勢呢！

➤ 應用練習

A	John, I'm going to need some time off. My mother just died.
B	Oh, I'm so sorry, Mary. Take as much time as you need.

A：約翰，我需要請幾天假。
我母親剛過世了。

B：喔，我很遺憾，瑪麗。
看你需要請多久就請多久吧。

A	John, I know that you are having problems at home. I appreciate you sticking it out here at work, but these problems have taken their toll on your performance. Why don't you take a few days to sort things out?
B	Thanks. You're right. I'll call you when things are better.

A：約翰，我知道你家裡出了點事。
我很感謝你繼續在工作崗位上盡力著，不過你家裡的
問題已經影響到你的工作表現。
為何不請個幾天假去解決它們呢？

B：謝謝你，你說的對。

　　事情好轉時我會打電話給你。

A
Excuse me, Mary.
I was wondering if I could take a couple of days
to move my grandmother into a nursing home.

B
Oh sure John.
I've gone through that before.
A couple of days won't kill us.
Take care of your grandmother.

A：不好意思唷，瑪麗。

　　我想知道我可否請幾天假把我祖母送到到養老院去。

B：喔當然可以，約翰。

　　我以前也碰過這種事。

　　幾天的假無可厚非。

　　好好照顧你祖母吧。

A
Mr. White, I wanted to ask you if I could take a
few days to sort out some family problems.
My son ran away from home.

B
God, that must be awful!
Yes, absolutely, take some time off.
I hope things work out.

A：懷特先生，想問你我可否請幾天假去解決一些家務事。

　　我兒子逃家了。

B：天呀，那一定很糟糕！
你當然可以請幾天假吧。
希望事情能解決。

單字銀行 Word Bank

Nouns 名詞

surgery	[ˈsɝdʒərɪ]	手術
cell phone		手機
performance	[pɚˈfɔrməns]	表現
nursing home		養老院

片語小舖 Phrases Shop

※ play it by ear
見機行事

※ sort out
解決事情

※ work out
事情獲得解決

UNIT 15 | I want to go on a vacation.

MP3-16

我要去度假。

課 前 維 他 命 Vitamin before class

忙碌的工作告一段落，只要是凡人都會想要拗個 vacation（假期）來休息一陣子吧？某人要放假，叫做 take one's vacation。A 先生要放假了，就說 A is taking his vacation，輪到 B 小姐想要放假，就變成 B wants to take her vacation。若是我已經放完假，那就是 I have taken my vacation。Got it?

▶ 對話一

A : Mr. Smith? Hello.

史密斯先生？ 哈囉。

I wanted to talk to you about my vacation time.

我想跟你談談休假的時間。

B : What about it?

怎麼回事呢？（請說）

A : Well, I'm not scheduled for a vacation for another two months, but I was wondering if I could take it next month.

接下來的兩個月，我並沒有排休假，但是我想知道我下個月可不可以休假。

My wife's vacation is next month.

我太太的休假是在下個月。

B : Well, I suppose that would be all right.

嗯，我想應該可以。

Just let me know sooner next time all right?

下一次早點讓我知道，好嗎？

A : I will, sir. Thank you.

我會的，老闆。 謝謝你。

➤ 對話二

A : You wanted to talk to me, John?

你想找我談嗎，約翰？

B : Yes, Ms. Frost.

是的，佛羅斯小姐。

I was hoping I could take my vacation time this June.

我希望今年六月能夠休假。

A : I don't see why not.

我看應該沒有問題。

You've got two weeks coming to you, don't you?

你有兩個星期的假期，不是嗎？

B : Yes, ma'am.

是呀。

I'd like to go to Peru.

我想去秘魯。

A : Well, that sounds exciting.

嗯，聽起來滿讓人興奮的。

Yes, June is fine.

六月沒有問題。

➤ 應用練習

A Mrs. White, do you suppose I could take my vacation next week?

B I wish you wouldn't, with everything that's going on, but you can take it whenever you like.

A：懷特太太，你認為我下禮拜能休假嗎？

B：公司正忙著，我希望你不要下禮拜休假，不過你何時 想休假都可以。

A John, I'd like to take a vacation next month if that's all right.

B I believe Gary is taking his vacation next month, too.
I suppose that's all right.

A：約翰，如果可以的話我下個月想休假。
B：我相信蓋瑞在下個月也要休假。
　　我想那應該不成問題。

A Mr. Lee, would it be all right if I took my vacation in May?

B That would be fine.

A：李先生，我可以在五月休假嗎？
B：那沒問題。

A If I can finish this project by Friday, could I take my vacation next week?

B If you can finish this project by Friday, you can take an extra week for vacation.

A：如果我能在週五前把這個企畫完成，我下禮拜能夠休假嗎？
B：如果你能在週五前把這個企畫完成，你可以再多一星期的休假。

課後馬殺雞 Massage after class

by+ 時間，就是在某時間之前。by Friday，週五之前的意思。正在進行中的每件事，叫做 everything that's going on。我們曾在之前的單元學過，問人家近來可好，可以說：What's going on？也就是在詢問對方，身邊的事情進展的如何呢？日子進展的如何呢？

單字銀行 Word Bank

Verbs 動詞

suppose	[sə'poz]	認為應該 _; 猜想 _; 以為…

Nouns 名詞

vacation	[ve'keʃən]	假期
Peru	[pə'ru]	秘魯
project	['pradʒɛkt]	企畫

Adjectives 形容詞

extra	['ɛkstrə]	額外的

MEMO

CHAPTER 4

租屋英語

UNIT 16 | How do I get an apartment?

MP3-17

我怎麼找一間出租公寓？

課前維他命 Vitamin before class

快速租屋有撇步唷。只要找到 leasing agent（租屋代理商），they could probably find one quickly（他們可能很快就會找得到房子）。

➤ 對話一

A : Do you know where I could find a leasing agent?

你知道哪裡可以找的到租屋代理商？

B : There are several in town.

在城裡有一些。

A : Are there any that you would recommend?

你能推薦一些給我嗎？

B : Apartment Finders and Superlease are good.

公寓搜尋者跟超級租屋都不錯。

➤ 對話二

A : Do you know of any good apartments for lease?

你知道任何好的公寓出租嗎？

B : No, but if you call a leasing agent, they could probably find one quickly.

不知道，不過你可以打給租屋代理商，他們可能很快就會找得到。

A : Are they listed in the phone book?

他們有被列在電話簿裡頭嗎？

B : Yes, look under apartments.

有呀，看看公寓那部分。

課 後 馬 殺 雞　Massage after class

一般在美國租屋，租金因地區而異。若是你在紐約曼哈頓租房子，很可能一個月要花上台幣三萬塊才能租到一個小小的地下室呢。真是花錢又受罪。

如果你是在地廣人稀的美國中南部，那麼一個月三萬元台幣，就可以租到一個不錯的兩房一廳的公寓，而且大多數還配有冰箱和廚房設備。

單字銀行 Word Bank

Verbs 動詞

recommend	[ˌrɛkəˈmɛnd]	推薦

Nouns 名詞

leasing agent		租屋代理商
apartment	[əˈpɑrtmənt]	公寓
phone book		電話簿

MP3-18

UNIT 17 # What's the place like?

那個地方是什麼樣子？

課 前 維 他 命 **Vitamin before class**

你喜歡住 ground floor（平房）還是 high rise（高樓）呢？ Let's see what's available.（讓我們一起來看看有什麼在出租吧。）此外，也得問問自己，How much would be your limit?（ 你的上限是多少租金呢？）

> **對話一**

A : Hello my name is Bob and I'm looking for a one-bedroom apartment.

哈囉，我叫做鮑伯。我正在找一房的公寓。

B : Ground floor or high rise?

平房式的還是高樓式的？

A : Ground floor with a pool, please.

有游泳池的平房式的。

B : What part of town are you looking for?

你在找哪一區的？

A : North Dallas.

　　北達拉司。

B : There are several available, sir.

　　先生，有好幾個你可以租的。

➤ 對話二

A : I'm looking for an apartment.

　　我在找公寓。

B : And what price range would you be looking for?

　　你在找什麼樣的價位的？

A : $1500 a month would be my limit.

　　最多是美金一千五百元一個月。

B : And how many rooms would you need?

　　你需要幾間房間？

A : Three bedrooms, two baths.

　　三間房間，兩間浴室。

B : Let's see what's available.

　　我們來看看有什麼在出租。

➤ 應用練習

A Does that rent cover any bills?

B The $800 pays for your rent and cable only.
You pay for electricity, water and gas.

A：這個租金包括什麼費用嗎？
B：八百元是付房租和有線電視而已。
　　你要自己付電費、水費和瓦斯。

A Are there any grocery stores nearby?

B Albertson's is two blocks away.

A：這附近有雜貨店嗎？
B：艾伯森超市離這裡兩個街段。

A Does this apartment have utility hookups?

B There are hookups for washer and dryer.

A：這個公寓有什麼設施的連接管嗎？
B：有給洗衣機和烘乾機的連接管。

A Are there any schools nearby?

B No, ma'am, this is the downtown area.

A：附近有學校嗎？

B：沒有，這是市中心區。

課後馬殺雞 Massage after class

美國房東（landlord）大致有兩種。第一種是喜歡把房租（rent）、水電（water and electricity）、瓦斯（gas）、有線電視和網路（cable）等費用通通算在一起，另一種就是會堅持把房租和其他各項費用分開來算。以美東地區為例，冬有冰雪夏有熱浪，開暖氣或是開冷氣都會特別耗電，所以有些房東傾向於把房租和水電分開來算。另外，有些房東並不提供冰箱以及家具，所以租房子的時候，一定要貨比三家算清楚，才能租到『經濟套房』。

單字銀行 Word Bank

Nouns 名詞

ground floor		平房
high rise		高樓
limit	[ˈlɪmɪt]	限度；極限
rent	[rɛnt]	租金
bill	[bɪl]	費用
cable	[ˈkebl̩]	有線電視
gas	[gæs]	瓦斯
grocery store		雜貨店
block	[blɑk]	街區
utility	[juˈtɪlətɪ]	生活設施
hookup	[ˈhʊkˌʌp]	連接管；連接線路
washer	[ˈwɑʃɚ]	洗衣機
dryer	[ˈdraɪɚ]	烘乾機
downtown	[ˈdaʊnˈtaʊn]	市中心區

Adjectives 形容詞

available	[əˈveləbl̩]	有空的，可出租的

UNIT 18 | How many bedrooms do you want?

你要幾間房的？

 **Vitamin before class**

相信大家都知道『公寓』叫做 apartment，在美國，尤其是美國南方，出租公寓很少獨棟的，大都是近百間公寓或是幾十間公寓一起，自成一個公寓出租區，這樣一個區屬於一個房東，當然囉，房東大半是專門從事公寓出租的公司，這樣一個公寓出租區，英語叫做 an apartment complex。

> **對話一**

A： I'd like an apartment like yours.

我喜歡一間像你這間的公寓。

How did you find it?

你怎麼找到的？

B： My boss referred me to the manager of this complex.

我的老闆介紹我來找這公寓出租區的經理。

A： Do you think there's anything here I would like?

你想這裡會有我喜歡的嗎？

B ： How many bedrooms do you want?

　　你要幾房的呢？

A ： Three bedrooms and a den.

　　三個臥房加一個小客廳。

B ： I believe there's one available on the east side of the complex.

　　我相信我們這公寓出租區的東側有一間正在出租。

課後馬殺雞　Massage after class

本單元裡所提到的 den, 在這裡當作『小客廳』解釋。一般美國的房子，都會有兩個客廳，den 通常就在一進門的地方，美國人會把它整裡的很雅致，平常生活起居不在這裡，den 是用來招待客人的，至於較裡頭的大客廳 living room 或 family room，是美國人平常看電視，生活起居的地方，通常只有和屋主比較熟的客人，主人才會邀他們進去。

➤ 對話二

A ： Do you know anyone who can help me get into this complex.

　　你知道有誰能協助我住進這個公寓出租區嗎？

B ： Well, that depends on what you're looking for.

　　那得看你要找什麼樣的房子。

A ： A one bedroom, something small.

只要一間房間的公寓，小小的就行。

B ： We can go talk to the leasing agent, Timothy.

我們可以去問租屋經理人，提摩斯。

➤ 應用練習

A What kind of a place are you looking for?

B I want something roomy with a fireplace.

A：你在找什麼樣的地方？
B：我要房間大一點，有壁爐的。

A I'd like to find a second-story apartment.

B Why?
You have to climb stairs if you live on the second floor.

A：我想要找一間二樓的公寓。
B：為什麼呢？
如果你住在二樓，你得爬樓梯。

A I'd like to get something close to your apartment.

B I think I saw a "for lease" sign on a townhouse right down the road from me.

A：我想要找一間靠近你公寓的住處。

B：我想在我住的地方下去的路上，我有看到一間房子，有要出租的牌子。

A I've got a dog now, do you know how much space I should look for?

B Your first hurdle will be finding an apartment complex that allows pets.

A：我現在養有一隻狗，你知道我應該找多大的地方嗎？

B：你第一個難處就是要找一個允許養寵物的公寓。

單字銀行 Word Bank

Verbs 動詞

refer	[rɪˈfɝ]	指點

Nouns 名詞

manager	[ˈmænədʒɚ]	經理
complex	[ˈkɑmplɛks]	（類似建築物一起的）一區
den	[dɛn]	小客廳
fireplace	[ˈfaɪrˌples]	壁爐
hurdle	[ˈhɝdl̩]	障礙；困難
pet	[pɛt]	寵物

UNIT 19 I'm not going any higher than that.

我最多只能出這麼多錢。

課 前 維 他 命 Vitamin before class

本單元要提醒您，租房子時一定要記得寫租約。因為租約能夠保障房東與房客雙方。英文裡，寫租約叫做 write up the lease。

➤ 對話一

A : Since the foundation is cracked, I'd like a discount on the price.

既然地基有裂開，價錢上你要給我打個折扣。

B : How much of a discount do you think would be fair?

你認為折扣多少是合理？

A : $300 a month.

一個月少收三百元。

B : I think that's a little steep.

我認為那太多了。

How about $150?

一百五十元怎麼樣？

A : That's fine I guess.

我想可以。

B : I'll write up the lease.

我來寫租約。

➤ 對話二

A : Without a pet deposit, you'd have to sign a two-year lease.

沒有寵物保證金，你必須簽兩年的租約。

B : How much is the pet deposit?

寵物保證金要多少錢？

A : Three hundred dollars, non-refundable.

三百元，不退的。

B : How about a one-year lease, with a $150 pet deposit?

我簽一年租約，給個一百五十元寵物保證金怎麼樣？

A : That will be fine, but I'll have to increase your rent slightly.

那可以，但是租金要加一點。

B : Fine, just write it up.

好，把租約準備好吧。

➤ 應用練習

A How soon can I move in?

B Three weeks with a deposit today.

A：我多快可以搬進來？
B：今天付訂金，三星期後可以搬進來。

A Is there any chance I could wave the security deposit?

B I'll ask my manager.

A：我可不可以不用付保證金？
B：我得問問經理。

A I really like this place, but I feel the rent you're asking for is a little expensive.

B I'm sorry, ma'am, I don't determine the price. The owner feels it is worth it.

A：我真的很喜歡這個地方，但是我覺得你要的租金貴了
　　一點。
B：小姐，我很抱歉，但是租金不是我訂的。
　　屋主認為值這個價錢。

A Could I lower my monthly rent by signing a three-year lease?

B I could probably do that for a five-year lease, but nothing less.

A：我簽三年合約，每月租金可以低一點嗎？

B：五年租約，我可以減房租，少於五年就不行。

課後馬殺雞 Massage after class

出門在外，能有個地方『睡』是最重要的。對於窮留學生來說，租個單人房就綽綽有餘了。一般而言，房東都會提供書桌，床、床墊（mattress），以及衣櫥（closet)，至於其他的，就要自己買了。在美國有一種東西叫做 davenport, 指的是坐臥兩用的長沙發。另外 hide-away-bed 則是一種可拉出的沙發床。

單字銀行 Word Bank

Verbs 動詞

crack	[kræk]	裂開
increase	[ɪnˈkris]	增加
determine	[dɪˈtɝmɪn]	決定

Adverbs 副詞

slightly	[ˈslaɪtlɪ]	輕微的；少許的

Nouns 名詞

foundation	[faʊnˈdeʃən]	地基；基礎
discount	[ˈdɪskaʊnt]	折扣
pet deposit		寵物保證金
security deposit		保證金

Adjectives 形容詞

steep	[stip]	價格過高的
non-refundable		不能退還的

MEMO

CHAPTER 5

談論選舉

UNIT 20 | What are the candidates like?

這些候選人都是怎麼樣？

課 前 維 他 命 Vitamin before class

有看過美國電影『白宮夜未眠』(The American President) 嗎？這可以說是一部成人版的『仙履奇緣』。片中的女主角 Sidney 是環保團體的說客，她的工作是來說服美國總統，推動通過環保法案。沒料到這位美麗的說客，竟讓帥氣的總統（麥克道格拉斯飾演）一見傾心，落入情網。堂堂美國總統為了追求心儀的女子，也有不知所措的一面。他打電話到花店去訂花，店裡的小妹聽到他說：『我是總統』，就把電話掛了。（如果你是花店小妹，你大概也會以為這是個惡作劇（a practical joke）吧。對於『白宮』（White House）有興趣的讀者，不妨看看這部浪漫愛情片。

➤ 對話一

A : Do you think Mr. Smith is reputable?

你認為史密斯先生的聲譽好嗎？

B : Well, he has won several humanitarian awards.

嗯，他得過好幾個人道主義獎。

A ： What about the other candidates?

其他的候選人呢？

B ： I've heard some good, some bad, just like every election.

我聽說一些好的，一些不好的，就像每一次的選舉一樣。

▶ 對話二

A ： What do you think of Mr. Smith?

你覺得史密斯先生怎麼樣？

B ： I think his views are too conservative.

我覺得他的看法太保守。

A ： What do you think of Mr. Mayer, then?

那你認為梅爾先生怎麼樣？

B ： Well, he's not too great, either.

他也不怎麼好。

In my opinion, though, he's still the lesser of two evils.

以我的看法，他仍然是兩個爛蘋果中較不爛的。

> **應用練習**

A Did you hear the debates last night?

B I did. I liked the democratic candidate.

A：你有沒有聽昨晚的辯論？

B：聽了，我喜歡民主黨候選人。

A What do you know about the independent candidate?

B Well, his business grossed over ten billion last year.

A：你對這個無黨無派的候選人知道多少？

B：嗯，他的生意去年總收入超過一百億。

A White seems to be doing well in the polls.

B He'll never beat the republican.

A：懷特在民意調查中似乎很不錯。

B：他絕不可能打敗共和黨。

課後馬殺雞 Massage after class

赫赫有名的美國白宮位於華盛頓 D.C.（華盛頓特區）。每年三月下旬，是華盛頓 D.C. 的櫻花季。

單字銀行 Word Bank

Nouns 名詞

humanitarian	[hju,mænə'tɛrɪən]	人道主義者
humanitarian award		人道主義獎
candidate	['kændədet]	候選人
election	[ɪ'lɛkʃən]	選舉
debate	[dɪ'bet]	辯論
poll	[pol]	民意調查
republican	[rɪ'pʌblɪkən]	共和黨
democratic candidate		民主黨候選人
independent candidate		無黨派候選人

Adjectives 形容詞

reputable	['rɛpjətəbl̩]	受好評的；聲譽佳的
democratic	[,dɛmə'krætɪk]	民主的
independent	[,ɪndɪ'pɛndənt]	無黨派的

UNIT 21 | Who are you going to vote for?

MP3-22

你要投票給誰？

課前維他命 Vitamin before class

你知道有很多星星（star）與線條（stripe）的美國國旗要怎麼說嗎？

答案是 The Stars and the Stripes.

> **對話一**

A ： Who are you going to vote for?

你要投票給誰？

B ： I tend to vote with my party, and I'm a Democrat.

我想要投給我的政黨，我是民主黨。

A ： So you'll be voting for Jensen then?

那麼你是要投給傑森了？

B ： He's no worse than any other politician.

他不比其他的政治家差。

➤ 對話二

A : I think I'll vote for the republican.

我想我要投給共和黨員。

B : Why would you do that?

你為什麼要那麼做？

A : I come from a long line of Republicans.

我是來自共和黨家庭。

B : And do you like this candidate?

你喜歡這個候選人嗎？

A : Not in particularly.

不是特別喜歡。

B : I would reevaluate the candidates if I were you.

如果我是你，我會再評估這些候選人。

➤ 應用練習

A Come on, let's just vote democratic.

B Forget it, I like the independent guy.

A：好了，我們就投民主黨吧。

B：免談，我喜歡這個無黨無派的傢伙。

A What's the difference between republican and democratic?

B Their views on government.

A：共和黨和民主黨有何不同？

B：這兩個政黨的不同，在他們對政體的看法。

A I'm thinking of not voting.

B Then don't complain about the state of the country for the next four years.

A：我在考慮不去投票。

B：那未來的四年你就不要抱怨國家的情況。

A Even though I'm a democrat, I like the republican candidate.

B Well, you've got to go with the candidate you feel is best.

A：雖然我是民主黨，但是我喜歡這個共和黨候選人。

B：哪，你應該投給你覺得最好的候選人。

課 後 馬 殺 雞 Massage after class

我們都知道白宮叫做 White House, 美國的立法機構是 congress（國會），它包括 Senate（參議院），它的成員叫做 senator（參議員）和 The House of Representatives（眾議院），它的成員叫做 congressman（國會議員）。

單字銀行 Word Bank

Verbs 動詞

reevaluate	[ˌrɪɪˈvæljʊˌet]	重新評估

Adverbs 副詞

particularly	[pɚˈtɪkjələ˞lɪ]	特別地

Nouns 名詞

democrat	[ˈdɛməˌkræt]	民主黨員
politician	[ˌpɑləˈtɪʃən]	政治家

MEMO

CHAPTER 6

辦公室英語

UNIT 22 | I'm going to ask for a raise.

我要要求加薪。

課前維他命 Vitamin before class

你是個工作狂嗎？你經常 put in the time（投入時間與心血）嗎？有沒有人曾經稱讚你說：Your projects are top-notch.（你的企畫一流）呢？嘿嘿，一起來看看本單元的主角們在聊些什麼『辦公室知心話』吧！

➤ 對話一

A : John, come into my office for a few minutes.

約翰，來我的辦公室一下。

I need to talk to you.

我要跟你說話。

B : Certainly, sir.

好的。

What is it you would like to talk about?

你要談什麼？

A : I wanted to congratulate you, John.

我要跟你恭喜。

130

You are our employee of the month.

你榮獲本月優秀員工獎。

B : Really? That's wonderful! Thank you, sir.

真的？太好了。謝謝你。

➤ 對話二

A : What do you think my chances are of asking Bob for a raise?

你覺得我向巴比要求加薪的機會大不大？

B : Well, you've put in the time, your projects are top-notch.

嗯，你投入很多心血，企畫也是一流的。

I don't think it would be out of line to ask for a raise.

我不覺得你沒有要求加薪的資格。

A : Yes, but will he think so?

是呀，但是他會這麼想嗎？

B : Bob is a nice guy.

巴比是個好人。

Sure he's a little rough around the edges, but he knows what an asset you are to this company.

當然啦他有點不好惹，不過他知道你是公司的一項資產。

Just talk to him about it.

就跟他談談看吧。

➤ 應用練習

A Hey, did you see this new job posting for a technical writer?

B Yes, I put it up.
We really need someone qualified to write textbooks for our telecommunications classes.

A：嘿，你有看到這份招募科技作者的新工作嗎？

B：是呀我提上去的。
我們確實需要一個適當的人來幫我們的電信學課程寫一些教材。

A John, I could really use some help on this project.
Do you have the time?

B Sure Jane.
Let me take a look at what you've done.
I'll get back to you before the meeting.

A：約翰，這份企畫我確實需要協助。
你有空嗎？

B：有，珍。
讓我看看你做了什麼。
我會在會議前給你回覆。

課 後 馬 殺 雞 Massage after class

我們以前學過的 raise 是個動詞，當作『提高』『養育』的意思。
本單元中，認真工作的男主角想跟上司 Bob 要求加薪，此時，
raise 就當作名詞用，變成『加薪』的意思。你也想要 ask for a
raise（要求加薪）嗎？

單字銀行 Word Bank

Nouns 名詞

emergency	[ɪˈmɚdʒənsɪ]	緊急
account	[əˈkaʊnt]	帳目
raise	[rez]	加薪
asset	[ˈæsɛt]	資產
telecommunication	[ˈtɛləkəˌmjunəˈkeʃən]	電信學

Adjectives 形容詞

top-notch	[ˈtapˈnatʃ]	第一流的；最高級的
technical	[ˈtɛknɪkl̩]	科技的

片語小舖 Phrases Shop

❀ put in the time
　投入時間

MEMO

UNIT 23 · We're having a meeting today.

MP3-24

我們今天有個會議。

課前維他命 Vitamin before class

現代人生活忙碌，無論是芝麻小事還是國家大事，總讓人喘不過氣。此時，隨身攜帶 memo（備忘錄），隨時記下重要事項，保證讓你頭腦清醒，無往不利。memory 是記憶力的意思，memo 則是幫助你記憶的好工具。現在很流行的 PDA（personal device assistant）就是一種掌上型個人數位助理，也就是所謂的電子備忘錄。

➤ 對話一

A : Miss Jones, I need you to take a memo.

瓊斯小姐，我需要你做一份備忘錄。

B : Certainly Mr. Lee.

好的，李先生。

A : And could you ask the executive director to come by when he has a chance?

你能問問執行長，若有機會能夠來一趟嗎？

B ： He's in a meeting right now, but I'll ask him as soon as he is free.

他正在開會中，不過我會在他有空時馬上問他。

> **對話二**

A ： Hi, you wanted me to pick up the Harper case?

嘿，你要我接哈波的案子嗎？

B ： Yes, thanks so much for helping me out.

是的，非常感謝你幫助我。

Here are all the files.

檔案都在這裡。

A ： Where are you in your negotiations?

你的協商進行到哪裡了？

B ： Not too far, that's why I feel okay in turning it over to someone else.

還沒什麼進展，所以我很放心把它移交給別人。

➤ 應用練習

A I've finished my brief.
Could you look it over?

B I'd be happy to, but I'm sure it's fine.

A：我已經完成了我的簡報。
你能幫我看看嗎？
B：我很樂意幫你看看，但我相信應該是沒問題。

A This summary is really good, John.
You're doing a great job.

B Thanks.
I couldn't have done it without your help.

A：約翰，這個總結做的很好。
你表現的很棒。
B：謝謝。
沒有你的幫忙，我也完成不了。

A I think that meeting was very productive.

B Yes, it really helps to get everybody's ideas out on the table.

A：我認為這次會議很有成效。
B：是呀，這次開會讓每個人的想法浮出檯面。

單字銀行 Word Bank

Verbs 動詞

research	[rɪ'sɝtʃ]	研究
insist	[ɪn'sɪst]	堅持

Nouns 名詞

memo	['mɛmo]	備忘錄
executive director		執行長
negotiation	[nɪ,goʃɪ'eʃən]	協商
brief	[brif]	簡報
stock	[stɑk]	股票

Adjectives 形容詞

productive	[prə'dʌktɪv]	有用的

片語小舖 Phrases Shop

❋ turn over
移交

CHAPTER 7

閒聊

MP3-25

UNIT 24 | How's he been doing?

他這一向好嗎？

課前維他命 Vitamin before class

太陽底下無新鮮事，不過，要是你聽到某個熟人很興奮地告訴你：Guess who I just ran into at the grocery store?（猜猜看我在雜貨店碰到誰？）想必他所碰到的人一定也是你失聯已久的對象。此時，你應該會很好奇那個人是誰，也想知道他的近況吧。

> ## 對話一

A : Have you heard from Chris since he moved?
打從克萊斯搬走後你有聽到他的消息嗎？

B : Yes, he called me last night as a matter of fact.
有呀，事實上，他昨晚打電話給我。

A : How is he doing in Seattle?
他在西雅圖一切都好吧？

B : He's a little homesick, but he said the new job is really great.

他有一點鄉愁，不過他說新工作很棒。

A : I just hope he's happy.

我只希望他能開心。

If you hear from him again, tell him to give me a call.

如果你有再跟他聯絡上，轉告他給我一通電話吧。

課後馬殺雞 Massage after class

本單元中的 Chris 自從搬去西雅圖後，開始有點 homesick（鄉愁）了。想家（home）想到生病（sick)，當然就是得了『鄉愁』啦。Homesick 也是許多海外留學生的共同體驗。一個人在異國孤軍奮戰的心情，確實不足為外人道也。另外，你知道 seasick 是什麼意思嗎？到了海（sea）上就生病，其實就是『暈船』的意思。凡是暈機、暈船、暈車，也可統稱為 motionsickness，亦即在移動（motion）中感到不舒服。

> **對話二**

A : Where is Joan?

瓊安在哪裡？

I thought she was going to join us for dinner.

我本以為她要跟我們去吃晚飯。

B : She called to say she had to work late.

她打了通電話說她必須加班。

A : Again?

又來了？

Man, she works some long hours.

嘿，她工作時間很長耶。

B : Well, when you own a business, you've got to put in time.

嗯，當你有自己的公司時，你得花時間投入。

> **應用練習**

A Have you seen Mary lately?

B No I haven't.
I believe she's busy taking care of her sick mother.

A：你最近有看到瑪麗嗎？

B：沒有耶。
我相信她正忙著照顧她生病的老媽。

A Guess who I just ran into at the grocery store?
Barry Sanders.

B You're kidding!
I haven't seen him since high school.

A：猜猜看我在雜貨店碰到誰？
　　貝瑞山德。
B：你在說笑吧！
　　從高中起我就沒看過他了。

A I heard Robert is getting divorced.

B Oh that's terrible.
Maybe we should drop by his house and see
how he's doing.

A：我聽說羅伯特要離婚了。
B：喔，真糟糕。
　　也許我們應該去他家看看他好不好。

A Sherry said she's going to take the manager job.

B Oh I'm glad.
She'll do great in that position.

A：雪瑞說她要接受那個經理職位。
B：喔我真高興。
　　她在那個職位會表現突出的。

單字銀行 Word Bank

Nouns 名詞

business	[ˈbɪznɪs]	商業;事業

Adjectives 形容詞

homesick	[ˈhomˌsɪk]	鄉愁
divorced	[dəˈvorst]	離婚
terrible	[ˈtɛrəbl̩]	糟糕的

片語小舖 Phrases Shop

❋ as a matter of fact
　事實上

❋ run into
　偶然遇到…

UNIT 25 Where are you going on vacation?

MP3-26

你要去哪裡度假?

課前維他命 Vitamin before class

有聽過『萬里尋親』的故事嗎?本單元裡的主角打算利用難得的假期去遙遠的義大利找親戚呢!你知道『遠在天邊』的英文要怎麼說嗎? Somewhere near the mountain.

▶ 對話一

A : What will you do on your vacation?
你放假時要幹嘛呢?

B : I'm thinking of going to Italy to find my relatives.
我正在考慮去義大利找我的親戚。

A : Wow, you have relatives in Italy?
哇,你在義大利有親戚?

B : Yes, somewhere near the mountains.
是呀,遠在天邊的親戚。
I've never met them.
我從未見過他們。

➤ 對話二

A : Are you looking forward to your vacation?
你期待著你的假期嗎？

B : Yes, I am.
是呀，我是。

I haven't taken one in three years.
三年來我還沒有休過假。

A : Where are you going?
你要去哪裡？

B : I'm going to Vale, Colorado for some skiing.
我要去科羅拉多谷滑雪。

A : That sounds fun.
聽起來很有趣耶。

Have a great time!
祝你玩的愉快。

➤ 應用練習

A Only one more week until my vacation.
I can't wait.

B I know, I'm taking mine the week after you get back.
I need a vacation.

A：再一個禮拜我就放假啦。
我等不及了。
B：我知道，我會在你回來之後的那一週放假。
我需要假期。

A I heard you're heading to New York for your vacation.

B That's right.
I've never been.
I've always wanted to go there.

A：我聽說你要去紐約度假。
B：沒錯。
我沒去過。
我一直想去那裡。

A Don't you have some vacation time coming to you?

B Yes, ma'am.
I'm heading to Hawaii in two weeks.

A：你最近有沒有假期？
B：有呀。
兩個禮拜後我要去夏威夷。

A What do you think you'll do with your two-week vacation?

B I thin k I'll rent a cabin in the woods.
I'd like some peace and quiet.

A：兩個禮拜的假期你打算做什麼？
B：我想我會在森林裡租個小木屋。
我想要一些自我的時間和寧靜。

課後馬殺雞　Massage after class

in+ 時間，是未來式。in two weeks, 兩週後。

單字銀行 Word Bank

Nouns 名詞

relative	[ˈrɛlətɪv]	親戚
skiing	[ˈskiɪŋ]	滑雪
cabin	[ˈkæbɪn]	小屋

MEMO

UNIT 26 | Have you seen the news lately?

MP3-27

你最近有看新聞嗎?

課前維他命 Vitamin before class

數年前美國柯林頓總統的性醜聞你還記得嗎?你同意『道德責任』與『治國能力』是兩回事嗎?或者你只想說:It's the president's own business.(這是總統的私事)

> ## 對話一

A : What do you make of this Clinton/Monica scandal?
你對柯林頓與莫尼卡的醜聞有何看法?

B : I figure it's the president's own business.
我想這是總統的私事。

A : But what about his moral duty to the country?
但是他對國家該有的道德責任又該怎麼說?

B : There have been plenty of presidents who have cheated on their wives and run the country just fine.
有很多總統欺騙他們的妻子但還是把國家治理的很好。

課 後 馬 殺 雞　Massage after class

business 原是商業的意思。本單元中，business 指的是個人的私事，份內事，也就是別人管不著也不該管的事情。至於 Don't do any monkey business 這句話的意思，就是要你千萬別做不該做的事情。

➤ 對話二

A ： Did you hear about the escaped criminals?

你知道有罪犯潛逃了嗎？

B ： No, when did this happen?

沒聽説耶，何時發生的？

A ： Last night, three prisoners escaped the Reilly prison.

昨晚，三個犯人逃出瑞力監獄。

B ： You're kidding.

你在開玩笑吧。

I hope the police catch them.

我希望警察能逮住他們。

> **應用練習**

A　I'm so tired of hearing about Clinton and Monica.

B　Oh I know.
There have to be other things going on more important than the President's sex life.

　A：我已經聽夠柯林頓與莫尼卡的事了。
　B：就是嘛！
　　　應該有其他事情比總統的性生活更重要。

A　Did you know that they found some missing pages from Anne Frank's diary?

B　Yeah, I heard that on the news last night.
Pretty exciting.

　A：你知道他們在安法蘭克的日記中發現有些頁數不見了？
　B：是呀，我從晚間新聞看到了。
　　　真讓人興奮。

A I heard that Congress vetoed that healthcare bill yesterday.

B Oh really?
Well, I guess it was bound to happen.

A：我聽說國會昨天投票表決健保法案。
B：喔真的嗎？
　嗯，我想這是一定會發生的。

A Can you believe that O.J. got off?

B The whole trial was a mess – yes, I can believe it.

A：你會相信 O.J. 是沒罪釋放嗎？
B：整個審判過程一團亂呀，這個結果我相信。

單字銀行 Word Bank

Verbs 動詞

| figure | [ˈfɪgjɚ] | 猜想 |
| cheat | [tʃit] | 欺騙 |

Nouns 名詞

scandal	[ˈskændl̩]	醜聞
president	[ˈprɛzədənt]	總統
criminal	[ˈkrɪmənl̩]	罪犯
prisoner	[ˈprɪznɚ]	犯人
prison	[ˈprɪzn̩]	監獄
diary	[ˈdaɪərɪ]	日記

Adjectives 形容詞

moral	[ˈmɔrəl]	道德的
escaped	[əˈskɛpt]	潛逃的

片語小舖 Phrases Shop

❋ one's own business
　某人的私事

❋ be bound to
　一定會⋯

UNIT 27 | What's been happening lately?

MP3-28

最近有什麼事發生？

➤ 對話一

A : Saddam refused to let in the inspectors again today.
沙丹今天再度拒絕讓檢查員進去。

B : I hope that situation doesn't explode.
我希望事情不會鬧大。

A : I'm sure the government has everything under control.
我相政府能控制整個局面。

B : I guess.
我想也是。

But the threat of nuclear war makes me nervous.
不過核戰的威脅讓我很緊張。

➤ 對話二

A : I wonder if Bosnia will ever be at peace.
我懷疑波士尼亞能有和平的一天。

B ： Bosnia will probably achieve peace before Israel does.

波士尼亞可能會比以色列早日達到和平。

A ： You're right there.

你說的對。

It seems that the fighting will never end over there.

那邊的戰爭看起來永遠不會結束。

B ： I just hope that I live to see the fighting stop.

我只希望能在有生之年看到戰爭結束。

> **應用練習**

A Why isn't Clint Eastwood running for president?

B He's too busy making movies.

A：為何克林伊斯威特不參選總統呢？

B：他太忙於製作電影。

A What is wrong in the Middle-East?

B What isn't wrong in the Middle-East?

A：中東出了什麼事？

B：中東能有什麼好事？

A Who is that guy next to the president?
They don't let him speak much.

B That would be the vice president.

A：在總統旁邊的那個傢伙是誰？
他們不讓他多言。

B：那應該是副總統。

A If Nixon is not in politics anymore, why is he in
Newsweek ?

B I don't know.

A：如果尼克森不再參與政治，他為何會上新聞週刊？

B：我不知道。

課 後 馬 殺 雞 Massage after class

你知道有哪些小說與電影跟『戰爭』有關嗎？海明威的小說：
『戰地鐘聲』與『戰地春夢』都和戰爭有關。另外，電影『西
線無戰事』、『搶救雷恩大兵』、『英倫情人』等，也都是非常有
名的片子。

單字銀行 Word Bank

Verbs 動詞

explode	[ɪkˋsplod]	爆發；爆炸
wonder	[ˋwʌndɚ]	懷疑 _；想知道…
achieve	[əˋtʃiv]	成就…

Nouns 名詞

inspector	[ɪnˋspɛktɚ]	檢查人員
nuclear	[ˋnjuklɪɚ]	核子
fighting	[ˋfaɪtɪŋ]	戰爭；鬥爭
vice president		副總統
politics	[ˋpɑlətɪks]	政治

Adjectives 形容詞

nervous	[ˋnɝvəs]	緊張

CHAPTER 8

高科技

MP3-29

UNIT 28 | What is your e-mail address?

你的電子郵件位址是？

課前維他命 Vitamin before class

Hey, what is your e-mail address?(嘿，你的電子郵件位址是？)
你是不是每天都花很多時間在收發 e-mail 呢？有沒有網路購物
（shopping online）甚至是網路拍賣的經驗呢？喜歡上網的你，
快來看看本單元的會話內容吧！從此以後，你就知道『寬頻』、
『網路伺服器』、以及『電腦設計說明書』要怎麼說啦！

▶ 對話一

A : Does your computer have Internet capability?
你的電腦能上網嗎？

B : Yes, I have cable modem access.
可以，我有裝寬頻。

A : I haven't heard of that.
我沒聽過。

B : It's the latest type of Internet connection.

這是最新的網路連結。

The cable company offers it.

有線電視公司提供的。

You can access the Internet through your television cable.

你可以透過電視電纜連上網路。

➤ 對話二

A : What is your e-mail address?

你的電子郵件位址是？

B : It's Joe@hinet.net.

是 Joe@hinet.net.

A : Do you like America online?

你喜歡線上美國嗎？

B : Yeah, it's a pretty good Internet service provider.

喜歡，那是一個很好的網路上線服務公司。

> **應用練習**

A
I bought all my Christmas gifts this year over the Internet.

B
Me too.
I found some great gifts online, and I had them delivered to my family and friends.

A：今年我所有的聖誕禮物都從網路上買。
B：我也是。
  我在網路上發現了一些很棒的禮物，然後我要他們寄給我的家人跟朋友。

A
My son loves his new computer.
He has a lot of new games to play.

B
Just make sure his computer has child safety features to avoid undesirable information.

A：我兒子很喜歡他的新電腦。
  他有一堆新遊戲可以玩。
B：要確認一下他的電腦能不能過濾色情網站以避免不良資訊。

A The things this computer can do are amazing.

B You're telling me.
I do my taxes with mine.

A：這部電腦能做的事可驚人了。
B：可不是嘛！
　　我就是用我的電腦做我今年的稅單。

A How do you like your computer?

B I love it.
I got one of the Gateway computers.
They built a computer according to my
specifications and delivered to my front door.

A：你喜歡你的電腦嗎？
B：我蠻喜歡的。
　　我買的是一部 Getaway 品牌的電腦。
　　他們根據我的設計說明書組了一部電腦而且還送到我
　　家前門。

單字銀行 Word Bank

Verbs 動詞

deliver	[dɪˈlɪvɚ]	投遞；傳送

Nouns 名詞

cable modem access		寬頻
internet connection		網路連線
internet service provider		網際網路線路提供者
specification	[ˌspɛsəfəˈkeʃən]	設計說明書
front door		前門

Adjectives 形容詞

undesirable	[ˌʌndiˈzaɪrəbl̩]	不良的

MP3-30

UNIT 29 How do I get online?

我要如何上網？

課前維他命 Vitamin before class

你曾在網路上登錄過個人信用卡號碼嗎？你怕不怕信用卡號碼被盜用呢？在美國，如果想在網路上進行各種交易，登錄信用卡號碼是非常頻繁的事情。基本上，思想單純的老美並不會想到『被盜領』的危險性。或許正如單元中的主角所言，the Internet is as safe a place as anywhere else.（網路跟任何地方一樣安全。）

> ### 對話一

A : How can I get hooked up to the Internet?

　　我該如何連上網路？

B : There are a variety of ways.

　　有很多種方法呀。

　　You can get a phone modem or a cable modem or number of other connections.

　　你可以用電話撥接或是有線電視數據機，或者是其他的連結。

A : What's the difference?

它們有什麼不同？

B : Speed mostly and cost.

主要是速度，還有費用。

The faster the information comes in, the more expensive it is.

擷取資訊愈快，費用就愈高。

➤ 對話二

A : Could you fax me the text for review?

你能傳真複習卷給我嗎？

B : I can do better than that.

我會用更好的方法。

Give me your email address and I'll email it to you.

把你的電子位址給我，我會把它寄給你。

A : Oh that would be great. .

喔，那真是太棒了。

➤ 應用練習

A I don't have access to the Internet but I want my son to have some educational software.

B That's not a problem.
You can purchase encyclopedias on CDRom.

A：我不能上網，不過我希望我兒子有一些教育軟體。

B：那不成問題。
你可以購買百科全書光碟。

A I want the convenience of shopping online,
but I'm afraid of having my credit card number stolen.

B To tell you the truth, the Internet is as safe a place as anywhere else.
If someone wants to steal your credit card, they can do it at a restaurant just as easily.

A：我想擁有上網購物的便利，不過我怕我的信用卡號碼會被盜用。

B：告訴你一個事實，網路跟任何地方一樣安全。
如果有人要盜用你的信用卡，在餐廳裡他們也可以輕鬆地做到。

| A | I have made so many friends on the Internet chat groups. |

| B | Me too.
Just the other day, I was talking to a girl in Singapore.
Can you believe that? |

A：我在網路的聊天家族裡認識了很多朋友。

B：我也是。

就在前幾天，我跟一個新加坡女孩聊天。你相信嗎？

| A | The only thing I don't like about this computer is that there's no technical support if something goes wrong. |

| B | That's an excellent reason to get another one.
You can't afford to have your system crash and not have someone who can fix it for you. |

A：這部電腦唯一讓我不滿意的就是出錯時卻沒有技術支援。

B：這是換一部新電腦的絕佳理由了。

你負擔不起系統壞了，卻找不到人幫你修理電腦的情況。

單字銀行 Word Bank

Verbs 動詞

steal	[stil]	偷取；盜用

Nouns 名詞

variety	[vəˈraɪətɪ]	各式各樣
review	[rɪˈvju]	複習
software	[ˈsɔftˌwɛr]	軟體
encyclopedia	[ɪnˌsaɪkləˈpidɪə]	百科全書
convenience	[kənˈvinjəns]	便利性
Internet chat groups		網路聊天家族

Adjectives 形容詞

educational	[ˌɛdʒʊˈkeʃənl̩]	教育的
excellent	[ˈɛkslənt]	最好的；極突出的

MEMO

CHAPTER 9

生病

MP3-31

UNIT 30 | Do you have a fever?

你有發燒嗎？

> ➤ **實用句型**

◈ **I think I'm coming down with something.**

我想我被傳染了。

◈ **You must be catching a cold.**

你鐵定是感冒了。

◈ **I just don't feel good.**

我只是不太舒服。

◈ **I'm achy all over.**

我全身上下都在痛。

◈ **You feel like you have a fever.**

你感覺上好像是發燒了。

◈ **He's got the flu.**

他感冒了。

➤ 開口說英文一

A ： You don't look so good.

你看起來不太對勁。

B ： I think I'm coming down with something.

我想我被傳染了。

A ： Do you have a fever?

你有發燒嗎？

B ： No, I'm just achy all over.

沒有，我只是全身疼痛。

➤ 開口說英文二

A ： Mommy, I don't feel well.

媽咪，我覺得不太舒服。

B ： What's the matter, dear?

怎麼啦，親愛的？

A ： My throat hurts and my nose is stuffy.

我喉嚨痛而且鼻塞。

B ： You must be catching a cold.

你一定是感冒了。

單字銀行 Word Bank

Nouns 名詞

fever	[ˈfivɚ]	發燒
throat	[θrot]	喉嚨

Adjectives 形容詞

stuffy	[ˈstʌfɪ]	鼻塞的

片語小舖 Phrases Shop

※ come down with something
感染某種病

UNIT 31　My tummy hurts.

MP3-32

我肚子痛。

➤ 實用句型

◈ **My tummy hurts.**

　　我肚子痛。

◈ **Does your stomach feel hard?**

　　你的胃很難受嗎？

◈ **It hurts when you touch my stomach.**

　　當你摸我的胃時，它會痛。

➤ 開口說英文一

A : Mommy, my tummy hurts.

　　媽咪，我的胃在痛。

B : Let me see.

　　讓我瞧瞧。

　　How does it hurt?

　　有多痛？

A : It feels really hard.

覺得很難受。

B : I think you might just have gas.

我想你大概是脹氣吧。

➤ 開口說英文二

A : What's wrong, Scott?

怎麼啦，史考特？

B : My stomach hurts.

我的胃在痛。

A : Where does it hurt?

哪個部位在痛？

B : In the middle and on the side.

中間還有旁邊。

It really hurts bad when I touch it.

當我碰它時真的很痛。

A : Maybe we should take you to see the doctor, then.

也許我們應該帶你去看醫生。

單字銀行 Word Bank

Nouns 名詞

tummy	[ˈtʌmɪ]	肚子
stomach	[ˈstʌmək]	胃
middle	[ˈmɪdl̩]	中間的

MEMO

UNIT 32 | I have such a headache.

MP3-33

我頭痛。

➤ 實用句型

◈ **I have such a headache.**

我頭痛。

◈ **My head is throbbing.**

我的頭正在抽痛。

◈ **My head is killing me.**

我的頭會要了我的命。

◈ **I have a headache behind this eye.**

我頭痛的部位在這眼後方。

◈ **He might be getting a migraine.**

他可能得了偏頭痛。

◈ **I have a splitting headache.**

我有劇烈的頭痛。

➤ 開口說英文一

A： Is something the matter?

哪裡有問題嗎？

B： Yes, I have a throbbing headache.

是的，我的頭在抽痛。

A： Have you taken anything for it?

你有吃任何藥物嗎？

B： I took some Tylenol a minute ago but it isn't working.

一分鐘前我吃了一些 Tylenol 不過沒效。(Tylenol 是一種止痛藥的品牌。)

A： You probably need to relax for a while.

你可能需要休息一陣。

B： You're right.

你說的對。

I think I'll go lie down.

我想我要躺下了。

➤ 開口說英文二

A： My head is killing me!

我的頭痛真要命！

B : Did you bump it?

你撞倒頭了嗎？

A : No, I think I'm getting a migraine.

沒有，我想我得了偏頭痛。

B : I hate migraines.

我恨死偏頭痛了。

A : Me too and I get them all the time.

我也是，而且我總是偏頭痛。

B : Well, take some Tylenol and go lie down for a while.

嗯，服用一些 Tylenol，然後躺下來一陣子。

心靈點滴

Be mindful. Don't worry or fret.
要用心，不要操心、煩心

單字銀行 Word Bank

Verbs 動詞

relax	[rɪˈlæks]	放鬆
bump	[bʌmp]	撞到頭

Nouns 名詞

headache	[ˈhɛdˌek]	頭痛
migraine	[ˈmaɪgren]	偏頭痛

Adjectives 形容詞

throbbing	[ˈθrabɪŋ]	抽痛的
splitting	[ˈsplɪtɪŋ]	劇烈的

UNIT 33 | My throat hurts.

我的喉龍痛。

➤ 實用句型

◈ **My throat hurts.**

我的喉龍痛。

◈ **I think I'm losing my voice.**

我想我快失聲了。

◈ **I've got a sore throat.**

我喉嚨發炎了。

◈ **It hurts when I talk.**

當我說話時它會痛。

◈ **You sound hoarse.**

你的聲音啞了。

➤ 開口說英文一

A : You're quiet today.

你今天好安靜。

B : I have a sore throat.

我喉嚨發炎。

It hurts when I talk.

當我講話時它會痛。

A : Have you tried gargling with salt water?

你用鹽水漱口了嗎？

B : No, I haven't.

還沒有。

A : It really helps a lot.

這招很管用的。

B : Really?

真的嗎？

I'll go do that now.

我現在就去做。

➤ 開口說英文二

A : My throat feels so dry.

我的喉嚨好乾。

B : You sound hoarse.

你的聲音啞了。

Are you losing your voice?

你失聲了嗎？

A : I think I might be.

我想是吧。

My throat really hurts.

我的喉嚨真的很痛。

B : Well, stop talking.

別再説話了。

That only makes it worse.

那只會讓情況惡化。

單字銀行 Word Bank

Verbs 動詞

gargle	[ˈgɑrgl̩]	漱口

Nouns 名詞

voice	[vɔɪs]	聲音

Adjectives 形容詞

sore	[sor]	疼痛發炎
hoarse	[hors]	沙啞的

UNIT 34 My ear hurts.

MP3-35

我的耳朵在痛。

▶ 實用句型

◈ **I have an earache.**
　　我的耳朵痛。

◈ **My ears itch.**
　　我的耳朵好癢。

◈ **My ear hurts.**
　　我的耳朵在痛。

◈ **I can't hear.**
　　我聽不到。

◈ **His ears are plugged up.**
　　他的耳朵塞住了。

◈ **I got water in my ears.**
　　我的耳朵進水了。

➤ 開口說英文

A : What's wrong with the baby?

小嬰兒怎麼了？

B : He has an earache.

他耳痛。

A : Poor thing.

好可憐。

Does he have anything for it?

他有沒藥物可用？

B : Yes, the doctor gave me some drops.

有呀，醫生給了我一些藥水。

➤ 開口說英文二

A : Mom, my ears itch down inside.

媽咪，我耳朵裡面發癢。

B : You probably got water in them when you went swimming.

之前游泳時你可能讓耳朵進水了。

A : What should I do?

我該怎麼辦？

B : We need to clean them out before you get an earache.

我們必須在你耳痛之前把水清出來。

Give me a minute and I'll help you do it.

給我一分鐘，我會幫你的忙。

單字銀行 Word Bank

Verbs 動詞

itch	[ɪtʃ]	發癢

Nouns 名詞

earache	[ˈɪr,ek]	耳朵痛

片語小舖 Phrases Shop

✤ be plugged up
塞住了

UNIT 35 You're burning up.

MP3-36

你在發燒。

> ### ▶ 實用句型

◈ **I feel hot.**

我全身發燙。

◈ **You're burning up.**

你在發燒耶。

◈ **His face is pink.**

他的臉好紅。

◈ **Her eyes look glassy.**

她兩眼無神。

> ### ▶ 開口說英文一

A : I don't think Mary feels too well.

我不覺得瑪麗已經好了。

B : Why do you say that?

怎麼說呢？

A ： Well, her face is pink and her eyes look glassy.

嗯，她的臉很紅而且兩眼無神。

B ： I hope she's not getting a fever.

我希望她沒發燒。

➤ 開口說英文二

A ： Daddy, I feel hot.

爹地，我全身發熱。

B ： Goodness, you're burning up.

天呀，你在發燒。

You must have an awful fever.

你一定得了嚴重的發燒。

A ： Are you going to take my temperature?

你要幫我量體溫嗎？

B ： I certainly am.

那當然。

單字銀行 Word Bank

Nouns 名詞

Goodness	[ˈgʊdnɪs]	天呀
temperature	[ˈtɛmprətʃɚ]	溫度；體溫

Adjectives 形容詞

glassy	[ˈglæsɪ]	無神的

UNIT 36 | He is sick to his stomach.

MP3-37

他的胃不舒服。

➤ 實用句型

◈ I feel nauseous.

　　我感到噁心

◈ I think I'm gonna puke.

　　我想我要嘔吐了。

◈ He is sick to his stomach.

　　他的胃不舒服。

◈ She needs to vomit.

　　她需要吐出來。

◈ My stomach is upset.

　　我的胃很不舒服。

➤ 開口說英文一

A : I don't feel so well.

　　我覺得不太舒服。

B ： What's wrong?

哪裡不對勁？

A ： My stomach is upset.

我的胃不舒服。

I think I need to puke.

我想我需要去嘔吐。

B ： Go to the bathroom and I'll bring you some medicine.

去廁所吧，我會帶藥來給你。

➤ 開口說英文二

A ： Are you feeling okay?

你還好嗎？

B ： Not really.

才不好咧。

I feel like I'm about to vomit.

我覺得我快要吐了。

A ： What's wrong?

哪裡有問題？

Do you have the flu?

你得了流行性感冒嗎？

B : I don't think so.

我不覺得。

I've just been sick to my stomach all day.

我的胃痛了一整天。

單字銀行 Word Bank

Verbs 動詞

puke	[pjuk]	嘔吐
vomit	[ˈvɑmɪt]	嘔吐

Adjectives 形容詞

nauseous	[ˈnɔʃɪəs]	噁心的

心靈點滴

We should appreciate, cherish and cultivate blessings.

知福、惜福、再造福

UNIT 37 | I need to burp.

MP3-38

我需要打嗝。

➤ 實用句型

◈ I feel bloated.

我覺得胃很脹。

◈ I need to burp.

我需要打嗝。

◈ My tummy feels nasty.

我的肚子很不舒服。

◈ I ate something that didn't agree with me.

我吃錯東西了。

◈ I think I have gas.

我想我的胃脹氣了。

◈ I have heartburn.

我的胃灼熱。

➤ 開口說英文一

A : I feel so bloated.

我覺得胃很脹。

I must have eaten something that didn't agree with me.

我一定是吃了一些不該吃的東西。

B : Do you want a Tums?

你需要來個Tums嗎?(TUMS一種可咀嚼的抗胃酸鈣片。)

A : Yes, please.

好。

B : Here, this should make you feel better.

給你,它會讓你好過一點。

A : Thanks a lot.

真謝謝你。

B : No problem.

沒問題啦。

➤ 開口說英文二

A : What's wrong, John?

怎麼了,約翰?

B : My stomach hurts.

我的胃在痛。

It feels really tight.

它繃的緊緊的。

A : It sounds like you have gas.

聽起來，你是胃在脹氣。

You just need to burp.

你只要打嗝就會好了。

B : You're right.

你說的對。

I'd probably feel much better if I did.

如果我打嗝或許就好多了。

單字銀行 Word Bank

Verbs 動詞

burp	[bɝp]	打嗝

Adjectives 形容詞

bloated	[ˈblotɪd]	脹氣
nasty	[ˈnæstɪ]	不舒服的；不愉快的

UNIT 38 I hurt myself.

MP3-39

我受傷了。

> 實用句型

◈ **He fell down.**
他跌倒了。

◈ **She scraped her knee.**
她的膝蓋破皮了。

◈ **I hurt myself.**
我受傷了。

◈ **Alex got hurt.**
艾力克斯受傷了。

◈ **It's bleeding a little.**
它有點出血。

◈ **I've got a blister.**
我起了水泡。

➤ 開口說英文一

A : Why is Mary crying?

瑪麗為什麼在哭？

B : She fell down and scraped her knee.

她跌倒了而且膝蓋破皮了。

A : Is it bleeding?

有流血嗎？

B : Just a little bit.

只有一點點。

A : I'll get her a band-aid.

我會拿繃帶給她。

B : Okay, I'll tell her you're coming.

好，我會告訴她你要過來。

➤ 開口說英文二

A : Ouch!

噢！

B : What's wrong?

怎麼了？

A : My foot hurts.

我的腳受傷了。

B : What happened to it?

它怎麼啦？

A : I've got a blister.

起了水泡。

See.

你看。

B : Ouch is right.

哇真的耶。

That does look painful.

看起來很痛的樣子。

小測驗 Check List

scrape　　_____

blister　_____

打嗝　b_____p

bloated　_____

不舒服的　n_____y

單字銀行 Word Bank

Verbs 動詞

| scrape | [skrep] | 擦傷 |

Nouns 名詞

| blister | ['blɪstɚ] | 水泡 |

Adjectives 形容詞

| painful | ['penfəl] | 痛苦的 |

片語小舖 Phrases Shop

❋ fall down
　跌倒

UNIT 39 | I think her leg is broken.

MP3-40

我想她的腿斷了。

> ### 實用句型

◈ **Don't move her.**
　　不要移動她。

◈ **I think it's broken.**
　　我覺得她的腿摔斷了。

◈ **It's broke in two places.**
　　兩個地方摔斷了。

◈ **How are you healing?**
　　你恢復得如何？

◈ **My arm seems to be mending well.**
　　我的手臂似乎痊癒了。

◈ **How did you break your leg?**
　　你是怎麼摔斷腿的？

◈ **I fell of my bike and broke my wrist.**
　　我從腳踏車上跌落，手腕關節摔斷了。

> ## 開口說英文一

A : Ouch!
　　　噢！

B : What's wrong?
　　　怎麼啦？

A : My leg
　　　我的腿。

I think it's broken.
我想，它摔斷了。

B : Don't move.
　　　不要動。

I'm going for help.
我去找人幫忙。

A : Hurry!
　　　快一點！

It really hurts bad.
我快痛死了。

➤ 開口說英文二

A : What happened to your arm?

你的手臂怎麼了。

. . . .

B : It's broke in two places.

有兩處摔斷了。

. . . .

A : How did that happen?

是怎麼摔斷的？

. . . .

B : I fell off a ladder.

我從梯子上跌下來。

. . . .

單字銀行 Word Bank

Verbs 動詞

heal	[hil]	治療；痊癒
mend	[mɛnd]	痊癒

Nouns 名詞

wrist	[rɪst]	手腕關節

片語小舖 Phrases Shop

❋ fall off
跌落

....

═══════ 小測驗 Check List ═══════

治療　h_____l
痊癒　m____d
梯子　l_____r
手腕關節　w_____t

UNIT 40 My tooth hurts.

MP3-41

我的牙齒在痛。

> **實用句型**

◈ **My tooth hurts.**
　　我的牙齒在痛。

◈ **I broke my tooth.**
　　我摔斷牙齒了。

◈ **I have a terrible toothache.**
　　我的牙齒痛的要命。

◈ **My filling fell out.**
　　我牙齒的填料跑出來了。

◈ **It hurts when I chew.**
　　當我咀嚼時，牙齒好痛。

◈ **She's got a terrible cavity.**
　　她的蛀牙很嚴重。

◈ **He should see the dentist.**
　　他應該去看牙醫。

➤ 開口說英文一

A : Ouch!

噢！

B : What happened?

怎麼了？

A : My tooth just started hurting.

我的牙開始痛了。

B : Try chewing on the other side.

試著用另一邊咀嚼。

➤ 開口說英文二

A : It hurts really bad when I chew.

當我咀嚼時，牙齒真的很痛。

B : It sounds like you have a terrible cavity.

聽起來，你有嚴重的蛀牙。

You need to see the dentist.

你需要去看牙醫。

A : I don't want to go to the dentist.

我不要去看牙醫。

B : That's too bad.

那太恐怖了。

You need to have that cavity filled before it gets worse.

你得在蛀牙惡化前把洞補起來。

單字銀行 Word Bank

Verbs 動詞

chew	[tʃu]	咀嚼

Nouns 名詞

cavity	[ˈkævətɪ]	蛀牙；凹處
dentist	[ˈdɛntɪst]	牙醫

牙齒保健小撇步

一、 選擇保健牙刷：帶有柔軟圓頭刷毛的牙刷，或是電動牙刷

二、 選用含氟牙膏：用帶有氟化物的牙膏

三、 刷牙時先從牙齒內壁刷起，然後再刷牙齒外側

四、 刷牙不要太用力

五、 至少在早晨和睡覺前盡可能徹底刷牙，刷 2 ～ 3 分鐘

六、 每天可用舌頭清理器或者牙刷清理一次舌面

七、 每週使用兩次絲制牙線

八、 每半年到醫院作一次牙齒健康檢查

UNIT 41 | I've got to get a shot.

MP3-42

你必須要打針。

▶ 實用句型

◈ It's time for you to get your shots.

你該去打針了。

◈ He hates shots.

他討厭打針。

◈ I've got to get a shot.

我必須要打針。

◈ She needs her immunization shots.

她需要打免疫預防針。

◈ Mary needs a Tetanus shot.

瑪麗需要打破傷風疫苗。

▶ 開口說英文一

A : What's wrong?

怎麼啦？

B ： I have to get a shot.

　　我得去打個針。

A ： It's not that bad.

　　沒什麼不好。

B ： I know.

　　我知道。

　　I just hate them.

　　我只是討厭打針。

➤ 開口說英文二

A ： I have to take Alex to get his shots.

　　我要帶艾力克斯去打針。

B ： That reminds me, Jane needs a Tetanus shot.

　　這倒提醒了我，珍需要打破傷風疫苗。

A ： If you want, you can ride to the clinic with us.

　　如果你要去診所，可以和我們一起去。

B ： Okay, let's plan to go tomorrow.

　　好呀，我們就明天去吧。

單字銀行 Word Bank

Nouns 名詞

immunization	[ˌɪmjənəˈzeʃən]	免疫
immunization shot		免疫預防針
Tetanus shot		破傷風疫苗

片語小舖 Phrases Shop

※ get one's shots
打針

心靈點滴

To give is more blessed than to receive.
施比受更有福

UNIT 42 I itch all over.

MP3-43

我全身都癢。

➤ 實用句型

◈ **Mommy, I itch.**
　　媽咪，我發癢。

◈ **Don't scratch.**
　　不要去抓癢。

◈ **She is contagious.**
　　她會傳染的。

◈ **I see bumps all over.**
　　我全身都起了小腫塊。

◈ **I think you're coming down with something.**
　　我猜你被某種東西傳染了。

◈ **Let me see if you have a fever.**
　　讓我看看你有沒有發燒。

➤ 開口說英文一

A : Mommy, I don't feel good.
　　媽咪，我覺得不太舒服。

B : What's the matter, honey?
　　哪裡不對勁呀，心肝？

A : I'm hot and I itch all over.
　　我發熱而且全身發癢。

B : Let me see.
　　讓我看看。

　　You have a lot of bumps.
　　你起了好多小腫塊。

　　It looks like chicken pox.
　　看起來很像是水痘。

A : It itches.
　　好癢。

B : I know but try not to scratch.
　　我知道，但試著不要去抓它。

　　You'll make it worse.
　　不然情況會更糟。

➤ 開口說英文二

A ： Alex has the chicken pox.
艾力克斯得了水痘。

B ： John's never had them before.
約翰以前都沒得過水痘。

A ： Then keep away from Alex.
那他要離艾力克斯遠一點。

He's very contagious.
他會傳染別人的。

B ： I hope John doesn't get them.
真希望約翰不要得水痘。

單字銀行 Word Bank

Nouns 名詞

bump	[bʌmp]	腫塊
chicken pox		水痘

Adjectives 形容詞

contagious	[kənˈtedʒəs]	會傳染的

UNIT 43 | I have a cramp in my leg.

我的腿抽筋了。

➤ 實用句型

◈ I have a cramp in my leg.

　　我的腿抽筋了。

◈ She woke up with leg cramps.

　　她起床時腿抽筋了。

◈ I'm having stomach cramps.

　　我的胃在抽痛。

◈ I can't open my hand.

　　我無法打開我的手。

◈ My fingers are cramping.

　　我的手指頭在抽筋。

◈ John had muscle cramps from exercising too much.

　　約翰運動過度，肌肉抽筋了。

◈ **Try to relax.**

試著放鬆吧。

> **開口說英文一**

A : I can't open my hand.

我不能打開我的手。

My fingers are cramping.

我的手指頭在抽筋。

B : Give me your hand.

把你的手給我。

I will massage it for you.

我會幫你按摩。

A : Thanks.

謝謝。

That feels so much better.

感覺起來好多了。

B : How did your hand get so cramped up?

你的手怎麼抽筋的那麼厲害？

A : I've been writing for three hours straight.

我已經一連寫了三個小時的字。

➤ 開口說英文二

A ： What's wrong?

怎麼啦？

. . . .

B ： I'm having stomach cramps.

我的胃在抽筋。

. . . .

A ： Do you need to go to the bathroom?

你需要到浴室去嗎？

. . . .

B ： No, I've already gone.

不用，我已經去了。

. . . .

單字銀行 Word Bank

Nouns 名詞

cramp	[kræmp]	抽筋
finger	[ˈfɪŋɚ]	手指
muscle	[ˈmʌsl̩]	肌肉
massage	[məˈsɑʒ]	按摩（馬殺雞）

Adjectives 形容詞

straight	[stret]	不間斷的

MEMO

國家圖書館出版品預行編目資料

世界最強英文聽力會話 / 蘇盈盈著

-- 新北市：哈福企業，2021.5

面；公分 . -- (英語系列；71)

ISBN 978-986-06114-2-7（平裝附 MP3)

1. 英語 2. 聽力 3. 會話

805.188

英語系列：71

書名 / 世界最強英文聽力會話
作者 / 蘇盈盈
出版單位 / 哈福企業有限公司
責任編輯 / Jocelyn Chang
封面設計 / 八十文創
內文排版 / 八十文創
出版者／哈福企業有限公司
地址／新北市板橋區五權街 16 號 1 樓
電話／ (02) 2808-4587 傳真／ (02) 2808-6545
郵政劃撥／ 31598840 戶名／哈福企業有限公司
出版日期／ 2021 年 5 月
定價／ NT$ 330 元（附 MP3)
港幣定價／ 110 元（附 MP3)

全球華文國際市場總代理／采舍國際有限公司
地址／新北市中和區中山路 2 段 366 巷 10 號 3 樓
電話／ (02) 8245-8786 傳真／ (02) 8245-8718
網址／ www.silkbook.com 新絲路華文網

香港澳門總經銷／和平圖書有限公司
地址／香港柴灣嘉業街 12 號百樂門大廈 17 樓
電話／ (852) 2804-6687 傳真／ (852) 2804-6409

email ／ welike8686@Gmail.com
網址／ Haa-net.com
facebook ／ Haa-net 哈福網路商城

Original Copyright © 3S Culture Co., Ltd.